FAR-FLUNG ADVENTURES

Fergus Crane

FAR-FLUNG ADVENTURES

Fergus Crane

Paul Stewart & Chris Riddell

dfb

David Fickling Books

OXFORD · NEW YORK

A DAVID FICKLING BOOK

Published by David Fickling Books
an imprint of Random House Children's Books
a division of Random House, Inc.
New York

Originally published in Great Britain by Doubleday, an imprint
of Random House Children's Books, in 2004.

DAVID FICKLING BOOKS and colophon are trademarks of David Fickling.

www.randomhouse.com/kids

Educators and librarians, for a variety of teaching tools, visit us at www.randomhouse.com/teachers

Library of Congress Cataloging-in-Publication Data

Stewart, Paul.
Fergus Crane / Paul Stewart & Chris Riddell.
1st American ed.
p. cm. — (Far-flung adventures)
SUMMARY: Nine-year-old Fergus Crane's life is filled with classes on the school ship Betty Jeanne, interesting neighbors, and helping with his mother's work until a mysterious box flies into his window and leads him toward adventure.
ISBN 0-385-75088-9 (trade) — ISBN 0-385-75089-7 (lib. bdg.)
[1. Adventure and adventurers—Fiction. 2. Inventions—Fiction. 3. Pirates—Fiction.
4. Ships—Fiction.] I. Riddell, Chris. II. Title. III. Series.
PZ7.S84975Fer 2006
[Fic]—dc22
2005018478

Printed in the United States of America

10 9 8 7 6 5 4 3 2 1

First American Edition

For Anna - P.S.
For my mother - C.R.

GENERAL MONTMORENCY

FIRE ISLE

THE EMERALD SEA

JELLYFISH ISLAND

FAT RABBIT ISLAND

DOUGHNUT ISLAND

TEAPOT ISLAND

THE SCORPION ARCHIPELAGO

STARFISH ISLAND

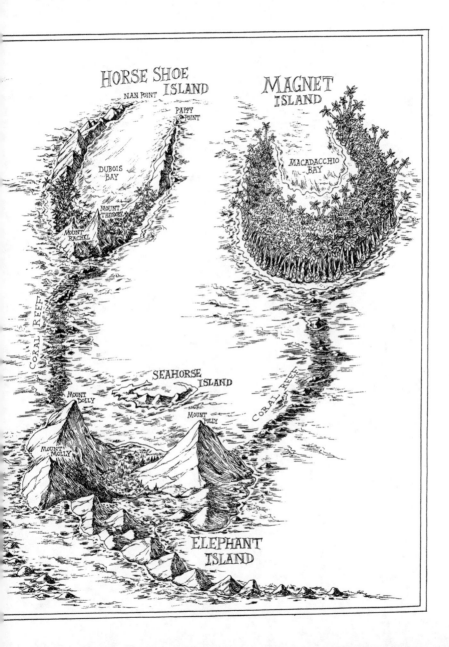

Chapter One

Your homework for tonight, me hearties . . . *erm* . . . I mean, children,' said Mr Spicer, absentmindedly playing with the large gold hoop that dangled from his left ear, 'is to read chapter thirteen of *Practical Pot-holing for Beginners*.'

The class gave a low groan.

Outside, seagulls flapped noisily round the returning fishing boats, while the coal barges moored to the quayside bobbed up and down on the light swell. Inside, the classroom of the school ship *Betty-Jeanne* was hot and stuffy and full of slowly nodding heads.

Will another one come tonight? Fergus Crane was wondering sleepily. And if it does, will I be able to stay awake long enough to find out?

The gently swaying classroom became hotter and stuffier than ever. Fergus's eyelids grew heavy. His eyes closed and . . .

'*Pffweeeeeep!*'

The shrill sound of the bosun's whistle echoed down the corridors, announcing the end of school. Fergus's eyes snapped open. It was four o'clock. At last! He was out of his chair and away before the whistle had even faded.

He didn't hear Mr Spicer telling the class that there'd be a test tomorrow; nor his friends calling their goodbyes; nor even Bolivia, the headmaster's parrot, squawking something at him as he ran down the gangplank. All Fergus could think about was getting home and waiting at his bedroom window for midnight.

Chapter Two

Fergus headed off along the canal. The heavy *Practical Pot-holing for Beginners* and his empty lunchbox bounced about inside the backpack on his shoulders; his shoes clattered on the cobblestones.

At the tall, pointing statue of General Montmorency, he turned left, and headed up into the labyrinth of narrow alleys. He hurried through square after familiar square, past fountains and sculptures, flower-stalls and candy-booths and small, candle-lit shops selling intricately carved wooden figures.

WALL-EYED NED

Turning right at Old Mother Bleeny's bagel-stand, Fergus emerged onto the bustling Boulevard Archduke Ferdinand, with its tall, slightly shabby buildings.

THE ARCHDUKE FERDINAND PLAYERS PRESENT "The Cycling Fish" A MUSICAL FARCE BY EDWARD T. TRELLIS Starring MISS EUGENIE BEECHAM AND SPECIAL GUEST APPEARANCE AS DAISY BY THE MIGHTY HANNIBAL!

Wall-eyed Ned was in his usual spot in front of the Archduke Ferdinand theatre. Head down, he was marching back and forth, the sandwich-board strapped to his body advertising the new show in town. This month it was a musical farce entitled *The Cycling Fish*.

'Afternoon, Ned,' Fergus called.

'Afternoon, Fergus,' Ned replied without looking up.

Further along the road, the air swirled with mournful music. Fergus smiled at old Antonio the hurdy-gurdy man, with his chestful of medals and curling moustache.

ANTONIO AND PEPE

5

His monkey, Pepe – dressed in a suit of red and yellow satin – jumped down from the wheezing barrel-organ and scampered towards Fergus. It seized the tasselled fez from its head, held it out upside-down and let out a little screech.

Fergus pulled out a handkerchief from his pocket, carefully unfolded it and presented an almond macaroon to the monkey.

'Bless you, my boy,' said Antonio and, for a moment, as Fergus continued, the slow mournful music speeded up.

He passed familiar shops. *Madame Aimee's Wedding Gowns. H.H. Luscombe's Umbrellas. Le Café Rondel. Joshua Berwick: Bespoke Tailor* . . . And as he hurried by, familiar faces appeared at the windows and waved or nodded. Everyone knew Fergus.

Beiderbecker's Bakery

Hannibal Luscombe saluted him with one of his umbrellas. Katrina – the waitress in *Le Café Rondel* – blew him a kiss. And, as he passed *Karpff*, the jeweller's, old Miss Wittering held up a half-eaten walnut eclair and winked.

WALNUT ECLAIR

ALMOND MERINGUE

Yes, everyone knew Fergus – he was Lucia Crane's boy, who sometimes helped his mother at Beiderbecker's cake counter. When they saw his face, Fergus's neighbours thought of glass counters full of cream-horns, or chocolate macaroons, or strawberry-slices, or best of all, *Archduke Ferdinand's Classic Florentines* . . . Little wonder they always smiled.

HAPPY BUN

SUMMER TART

At last, Fergus came to Beiderbecker's

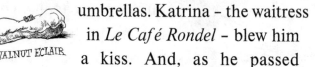

TRIPLE DECKER BEIDERBECKER
GATEAU

ARCHDUKE FERDINAND'S
CLASSIC FLORENTINE

BORIS BEIDERBECKER

Bakery itself. Boris Beiderbecker was a short, fat man with a large ginger moustache. He baked the bread – everything from plaited sourdough rye to malted wholemeal with a poppy-seed crust. Mrs Crane ran the cake counter.

Fergus pressed his nose against the window and peered through the displays of his mother's walnut eclairs and almond meringues at the counter. Sometimes she worked at the till in the afternoon. But not today. Apart from young Lucy, who was serving an old woman with a fat dachshund, the shop was empty.

Fergus turned away and headed for the doorway to the right of the shop. There was an arched plaque above the entrance bearing the words *Archduke Ferdinand Apartments*. Fergus thrust the larger of his two keys into the lock, put his shoulder to the heavy wooden door and shoved. The door opened with a creak and a sigh, and Fergus stepped inside.

The hallway was cool and fresh and, as the door shut behind him with a soft *click*, Fergus was struck by a heavy silence that seemed to press at his inner ear. It was like being under water. The next instant, he was struck by something else.

A smell. A *delicious* smell. The most wonderfully aromatic fragrance in the whole world!

'Florentines,' Fergus murmured.

Mrs Crane baked non-stop throughout the day. Croissants for the early-morning trade; cakes and pastries for lunchtime; scones, buns and multi-layered gateaux in the afternoon. But it was not croissants that Fergus could smell, nor warm spicy currant-buns . . . This was the unmistakable nutty, chocolatey, caramelly smell of the most delicious cakes ever created.

'Flo-ren-tines,' Fergus whispered slowly. Just the *name* in his mouth was enough to make his stomach gurgle with anticipation.

He closed his eyes.

He could see them floating before him – small roundels of toasted nuts, plump dried fruit, candy peel and glacé-cherries, all bound together with sweet, buttery toffee and set on a base of dark, velvety chocolate. He could almost *taste* them.

Fergus guessed that his mother must have been asked to stay late in the bakery kitchen to complete a special order.

He made his way across the marble hallway, past the row of metal letter boxes, their owners' names on the front of each little locked door. *Gumm. Bigsby-Clutterbuck. Squeegie. Beecham. Mme Lavinia. Fassbinder. Crane . . .*

Fergus stopped at the last letter box. A large parcel sat beside it, addressed to *Mrs L. Crane*. On one side was a sticky label with a picture of three penguins and the words *The Fateful Voyage Trading Co.* Fergus bent down and picked it up with a sigh. He wasn't the only one with homework. His mother was taking on more and more, just to make ends meet. Thank goodness the school ship *Betty-Jeanne* had offered him a free scholarship, Fergus thought, as he climbed the stairs.

It spared his mother the worry of school fees on top of everything else.

Taking them two at a time, Fergus hurried up the steep, marble stairs, pausing at the landings at the top of every second flight to catch his breath. There were two high-ceilinged apartments leading off each landing, one to the left and one to the right. Beside each door was a name-plaque which

MAJOR & MRS BARTHOLOMEW BIGSBY-CLUTTERBUCK

announced the identity of the person who lived inside. Some of the names were written by hand, some of them were printed.

Arturo Squeegie

On the first floor, there was Miss Jemima Gumm, who kept canaries, and Major and Mrs Bartholomew Bigsby-Clutterbuck and their Persian cat,

Miss Eugenie Beecham

Prince Caspian; Arturo Squeegie, who wore a black toupee, and his neighbour, Miss Eugenie Beecham, the famous actress, lived above them on the second floor, while Madame Lavinia,

a retired piano-teacher, and Dr Fassbinder, who taught at the Montmorency Academy, each had an apartment up on the third.

Half-way up the final flight of stairs, Fergus heard a sound behind him. He turned and looked back, to see Dr Fassbinder emerging from his

DR. FASSBINDER
Ba.(Msc)Olt.Cc.Sme.Od

apartment, dressed in a stiff collar and black bow-tie. In one white-gloved hand he was holding two

Dr. FASSBINDER

tickets to *The Cycling Fish*; in the other, his pocket watch.

'Botheration,' he muttered as he checked the time. 'Late again.' He put the two tickets in his waistcoat, and the watch in the inside pocket of his coat. 'I do hope I haven't missed the beginning.' And with that, he hurried off down the stairs, the steel-tipped heels and toes of his shoes clipping and clopping, quieter and quieter, as he went.

Fergus smiled to himself. Dr Fassbinder was *always* late for something.

On the fourth-floor landing, Fergus came at last to his own front door. It was smaller and scruffier than the others, and badly needed a coat of paint. The names *Lucia and Fergus Crane* were written in black ink on yellowed card below the bell. Fergus rummaged in his pocket for his keys.

Up here, directly beneath the sloping roof, there was room for only one rather small apartment. But as far as Fergus was concerned, it was the nicest, cosiest, snuggest apartment of them all – his mother had seen to that. She had the knack of taking something old or broken or unwanted and making it new again, with just a lick of paint or a carefully placed cushion or rug.

'If Archduke Ferdinand himself ever came to visit,' he used to tell his mother, 'then ours would be the apartment he would like the most.'

Fergus selected the smaller of his two keys and opened the door. A blast of air struck him in the face; it was deliciously warm after the chilly stairwell, and the wonderful, mouth-watering smell of Florentines which had accompanied him up the stairs abruptly grew more intense than ever.

Fergus had been wrong. His mother wasn't working late at Beiderbecker's at all; she was home early and baking him a batch of Florentines all of his own. And he knew what *that* meant.

'Is that you, Fergus?' Mrs Crane's voice floated out from the sitting-room. 'Good day at school?'

'Fine,' Fergus called back. 'Got some homework, though.' He tossed his backpack into the corner, crossed the hall and pushed the sitting-room door open. 'And so have you, by the look of it.' He held out the parcel.

His mother looked up as Fergus entered the room, pushed the strands of hair which had escaped from her bun away from her face and smiled a little sheepishly.

'Another one already,' she said. 'I hope it's as easy as the last batch. The money certainly comes in useful.'

Fergus nodded, and handed the parcel to his mother. He knew that the rent on the apartment was high; he knew that the wages Mr Beiderbecker paid were low. The extra work Mrs Crane took on meant they could just about afford all the basics, but there was precious little money left over. Fergus's jumper was already too small for him, and he hadn't yet told his mother about the hole in his right shoe.

Mrs Crane opened the parcel and a cascade of tiny paper horses tumbled out onto the floor, followed by dozens of paper wings and a printed note.

Dear Valued Worker, Mrs Crane read, smiling. *Please fix the wings to the horses by folding the tabs as instructed. No glue or paper-clips needed.*

Good luck and very best wishes, Finn, Bill and Jackson;

Vice-Presidents, The Fateful Voyage Trading Co.

Dear Valued Worker,
Please fix the wings to the horses by folding
instructed. No glue or paper clips

There was a P.S. *Pre-payment enclosed.*

'Look!' Mrs Crane cried, holding up a brightly coloured money-order. 'They've paid me already, and it's for . . . Oh, Fergus! Now I can afford to buy you a jumper *and* a new pair of shoes! I know you need some.'

'I like this jumper,' said Fergus, tugging the sleeves down to his wrists. 'And it's only a small hole. Honest.'

'You're a good boy,' said Mrs Crane, smiling, and added, 'I've baked you something special for tea.'

'You have?' said Fergus, feigning surprise. 'What?'

'Guess,' she said.

Fergus made a great show of closing his eyes, tilting his head back and breathing in deeply. 'It's nutty,' he whispered.

'Yes,' said his mother.

'Chocolatey . . .'

'Yes, yes.'

'Caramelly.' He gasped. His eyes snapped opened. 'It's not . . . is it? Archduke Ferdinand's Florentines?'

'It is!' said Mrs Crane gleefully. 'A special batch, Fergus. Just for you. My best boy.' She pushed back the strand of hair which had come loose again, and looked at him lovingly. 'They were always your father's favourites,' she added. Her gaze strayed over to the framed photograph on the sideboard.

Fergus looked too, and his eyes fell upon the familiar picture of the father he'd never known – a picture he'd looked at a thousand times before, studying every detail, looking for clues . . .

Marcus Crane was dressed in a naval uniform, with medals, gold buttons and tasselled epaulettes decorating the jacket, piping down his knife-edge trousers and a heavy peaked cap tipped at a jaunty angle on his head. At his belt, there hung a ceremonial sword on one side and a pistol on the other. He might have looked severe if it hadn't been for the look on his face – which was the image of cheeky-grinned, sparkly-eyed mischief.

Over the years, Fergus had asked his mother endless questions about the mysterious figure in the photograph, but all she would ever say was that he'd left on a voyage just before he, Fergus, had been born, and had never returned.

'I asked him not to go,' she would say. 'I begged him, but it was no use . . .'

And then she would begin to cry. Since Fergus didn't like to see his mother cry, he tried not to ask her too many questions – but sometimes he just couldn't help himself.

'Did you bake Florentines for him too?' he now asked.

'Oh, yes,' came the reply, and his mother sat back, a faraway look in her eyes. She didn't seem sad; just wistful.

'He brought me back macadacchio nuts from one of his voyages,' she said, her voice soft, reflective.

'Macadacchio nuts?' Fergus whispered, eager to hear more, yet terrified of breaking the spell that seemed to have taken hold of his mother as the memories came flooding back.

'Macadacchio nuts are the secret ingredient to the perfect Florentine,' she said. 'They're sweet but not *too* sweet; crunchy, yet they melt on the tongue, like honey mixed with sunlight.'

'Where do they come from?' asked Fergus tentatively.

'From a place called Magnet Island,' Mrs Crane told him, 'far off in the Emerald Sea.'

'Magnet Island,' Fergus repeated softly. 'The Emerald Sea . . . So my father sailed there? Who did he go with? And what was his ship like? Was he the captain? He's dressed like a captain in the photograph . . .'

Fergus knew he'd gone too far. His mother's face clouded over, tears welled up in her eyes. 'I *begged* him not to go . . .' she murmured.

Fergus jumped up and threw his arms around her in a big hug. 'Thank you for the Florentines, Mum,' he said.

Chapter Three

Fergus sat on the window ledge. At his feet lay a plate, a few Florentine crumbs and an empty glass. Beside them, a heavy clothbound book lay open at chapter thirteen – *Traversing Lateral Tunnels in Seven Easy Steps*. The clock in Montmorency Gardens had just struck nine, and downstairs his mother was still hard at work on the paper horses. Fergus pulled the quilt from his bed round his shoulders and settled down for a long wait.

The view from the attic window, high up above the city, was magnificent – a landscape of rooftops, chimneys and spires, in a patchwork of greys, purples and orangey-browns, all nestling at the foot of the mountains.

CHAPTER 13 – TRAVERSING LATERAL TUNNELS IN SEVEN EASY STEPS

Fig i.

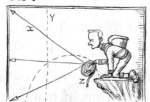

STEP ONE.
Ensure that all equipment is in good order and that an adequate length of rope for the procedure is available. To calculate length of rope required the following equation can be used:

Fergus sat there, patiently waiting as the sun set and the sky on the horizon became streaked with ribbons of orange and red. Slowly, the light faded, the stars came out, and between the buildings below him, Fergus could see the network of lamplit avenues and glinting canals which crossed and re-crossed one another in a series of bridges and aque-ducts. Far beyond, with the low full moon now reflecting on its choppy waves, was the ocean itself, rolling in from behind the horizon and slapping against the barnacled sides of the city's harbour walls.

And as he watched and his eyes grew heavy, it felt almost as though he were sitting at the bow of a great ship, about to slip its moorings and sail off across the moonlit ocean. Fergus leaned forward and breathed in the fresh night air.

He smelled sea salt, and the tang of beached seaweed; thyme from the foothills of the mountains, and the earthy chill of snow from their peaks. And, underlying it all, Fergus noticed as he closed his eyes and took the air deep down into his lungs, was the warm scent of fragrant spices wafting in from afar – cinnamon, nutmeg, vanilla, clove . . .

'One day, I'll leave the city and travel,' Fergus told himself. 'Over the mountains. Or across the sea . . .'

'The sea, the sea,' the air seemed to whisper, and Fergus found himself thinking of the photograph of his father – dressed up in his uniform. The hat, the sword, the smartly buttoned tunic . . .

His eyes grew heavy, his head began to nod. Suddenly, he sat up with a jolt. The clock had just struck twelve! He must have dozed off.

Fergus threw off his quilt and leaned out as far as he dared. Perhaps there wouldn't be one tonight

after all, he thought sleepily. He yawned, and was about to jump down from the window sill when something caught his eye. Fergus stopped.

He could just make out a dot, far in the distance, silhouetted against the large silvery disc of the moon. His heartbeat quickened. The dot grew larger and larger . . . He could see it clearly now – a small, silver box, with tiny feathery wings attached to its sides, beating for all they were worth.

'You've come back,' Fergus whispered. 'You've come back.'

Chapter Four

This was the third night in a row that the mysterious little flying box had arrived at Fergus's attic window. The first night he had been in bed, fast asleep, when he had suddenly been wakened.

Tap . . . tap . . . tap . . .

Fergus's eyes had snapped open. The tapping sound was coming from the window. He'd looked round to see the box perched on the narrow ledge outside, one of its mechanical wings knocking against the glass.

Fergus had climbed slowly out of bed, tiptoed across the room and nervously opened the window. The little box had flapped inside exhaustedly, its tiny wings beating in a curious up-down circular movement. Fluttering down, it had come to rest in Fergus's upturned hands.

Fergus had gently turned it over, marvelling at the little box's ornate carvings and perfect dove-tail joints. At the bottom was a gold key, slowly coming to a halt. As it had finally stopped, so the wings had also stopped moving. Fergus had gently placed the little machine on his quilt, and as he did so, a most surprising thing happened. A small door at the front of the box had sprung open, as if on a tiny spring, and out had popped a piece of paper. It was carefully folded and sealed with red sealing-wax, the imprint of a webbed foot pressed into its shiny surface.

Normally, Fergus wasn't the sort of boy to open other people's letters, especially when they were so carefully folded and sealed, but the strange mechanical box *had* tapped on *his* window, so perhaps this letter was meant for him. Fergus had rubbed the sleep out of his eyes, then carefully broken the seal and unfolded the tiny letter.

Dear boy behind the counter at Beiderbecker's Bakery, it read, in curling letters of jet-black ink.

The hairs at the back of Fergus's neck had tingled with a mixture of fear and excitement.

Please write your name in the box provided if you want to know something to your advantage,

Signed, T.C., a well-wisher.

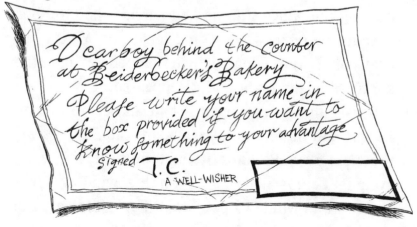

Fergus had looked at the piece of paper for a long time. It was certainly the strangest letter he'd ever received, and he wasn't at all sure he should reply to it. But whoever had sent the little box not only knew him as the 'boy behind the counter at Beiderbecker's', but was also clearly expecting a reply.

'It can't do any harm,' Fergus had said to himself. At that moment, the box had given a little click and a small silver pencil had popped out of its top.

'Here goes,' Fergus had said, taking the pencil and printing his name in full in the small box at the bottom of the letter. *Fergus Marcus Crane*. Then, before he'd had time to regret it, he had returned the letter to the box and wound the key up tight. Next, holding the wings still, he had carried the little box over to his open window and let it go. With a few beats of its tiny wings, it had flapped off into the darkness of the night and disappeared.

It was almost as though it had all been a dream, Fergus had thought in class aboard the *Betty-Jeanne* the next day. Perhaps it had, but the following evening Fergus had sat up on the window sill - shutters and window open - waiting, just in case the little box returned. He'd been on the point of giving up and going to bed when the clock in Montmorency Gardens had struck twelve, and he'd spotted it glinting in the moonlight, fluttering over the rooftops.

There had been a breeze blowing in from the harbour, sending wispy clouds scudding across the sky, and the tiny wings had fluttered desperately to keep the box on course. A number of times Fergus had thought it wouldn't make it, but it had bravely battled on until at last, almost with the last twist of its key, the little box had fallen into his outstretched hands.

'Got you!' Fergus had cried triumphantly, and then realized that he might wake his mother if he didn't keep quiet. He had placed the box on his quilt, the little door had sprung open and out popped a second letter.

Fergus had opened it with trembling fingers.

Dear Fergus Marcus Crane, it had begun.

Thank you for replying so promptly. Please tick the following boxes where appropriate. Thank you for your patience,

Signed, T.C., A FRIEND.

Fergus had read on as the little box gave a click and offered him its silver pencil.

Your mother's name is Lucia, it said. He had ticked the box marked 'yes'.

Your father's name is Marcus, the questionnaire continued. Fergus's heart beat wildly as, again, he had ticked the 'yes' box.

Next, asked whether he would describe himself as small, medium or large, Fergus had ticked 'small', thinking it best to be truthful. The following question was more specific. Was he agile, athletic, good at squeezing through small spaces, or none of the above? it wanted to know. Thinking of gym class on board the *Betty-Jeanne*, Fergus had ticked all the boxes except for the last one.

The final question was easy. *What school do you attend?*

Fergus had looked at the list of possibilities. *Montmorency Academy. Harbour Heights. The School*

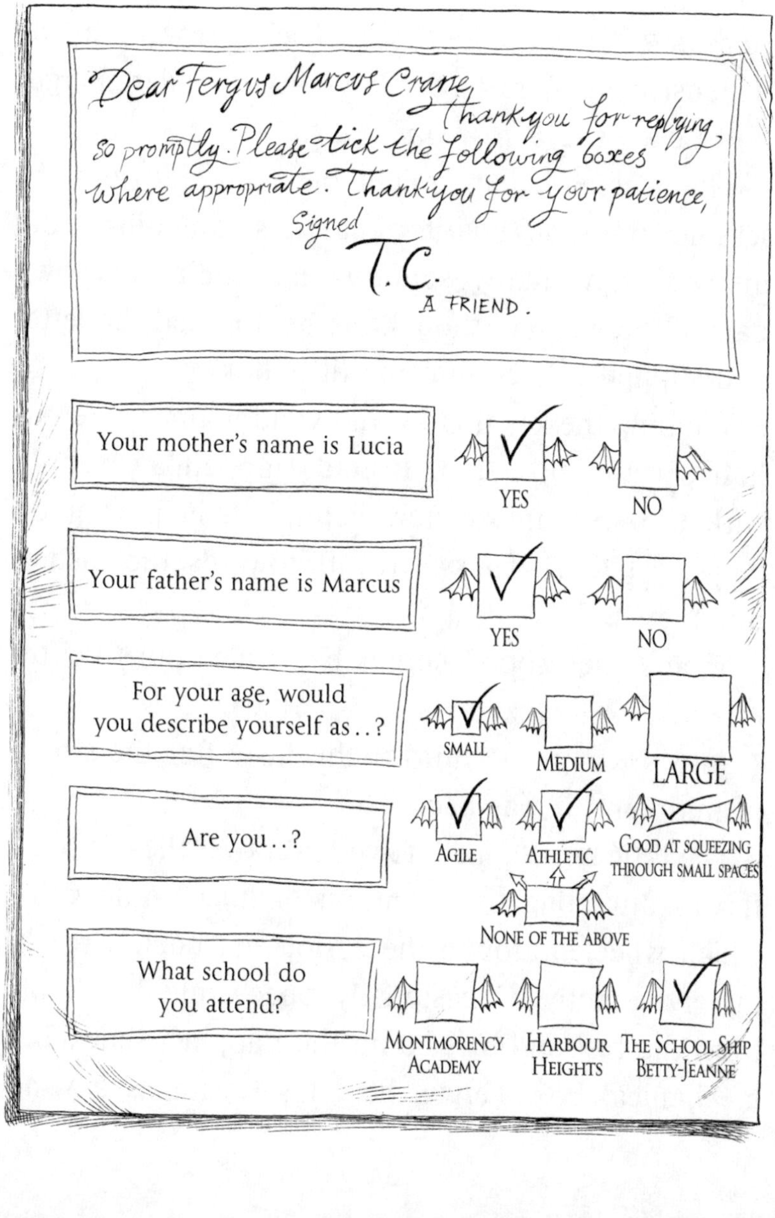

Dear Fergus Marcus Crane, thank you for replying so promptly. Please tick the following boxes where appropriate. Thank you for your patience,

Signed

T.C.

A FRIEND.

| Your mother's name is Lucia | ✓ YES | ☐ NO |

| Your father's name is Marcus | ✓ YES | ☐ NO |

For your age, would you describe yourself as..?

✓ SMALL   ☐ MEDIUM   ☐ LARGE

Are you..?

✓ AGILE   ✓ ATHLETIC   ✓ GOOD AT SQUEEZING THROUGH SMALL SPACES

☐ NONE OF THE ABOVE

What school do you attend?

☐ MONTMORENCY ACADEMY   ☐ HARBOUR HEIGHTS   ✓ THE SCHOOL SHIP BETTY-JEANNE

Ship Betty-Jeanne. The first two schools were far too expensive for Mrs Crane even to consider. Fergus had ticked the *Betty-Jeanne* box.

The teachers there might be a bit odd and the lessons unusual, but it didn't cost anything. And anyway, how many schools had their very own parrot? Fergus had thought as he'd folded the letter and slipped it back into the little box.

Winding the key till it would wind no more, Fergus had set the box free. It had flapped away and, with the stiff breeze now behind it, helping it on its way, had flown swiftly off towards the distant mountains.

'Come back soon,' Fergus had called quietly after it.

And now, on the third night, just after the stroke of midnight, it was back.

The little box flapped down lower over the rooftops. It was attracting the attention of huge white gulls, which wheeled around the curious intruder, screeching indignantly. Occasionally one would break off from the rest and dive-bomb the flapping, squeaking mechanical box. Fergus held his breath as a wing brushed hard against the box, knocking it off course.

'Come on,' he whispered encouragingly. The box righted itself. 'That's the way. Just a little bit further and . . . Gotcha!' Fergus's hands closed over the little box, and he could feel its tiny wings tickling his hands as he climbed down from the window sill. He placed the box on the quilt. As he did so, he noticed that one wing was crumpled and almost useless – battered by the white gulls. The little door opened and out fell another letter.

Fergus unfolded it eagerly. The next moment, his jaw dropped . . .

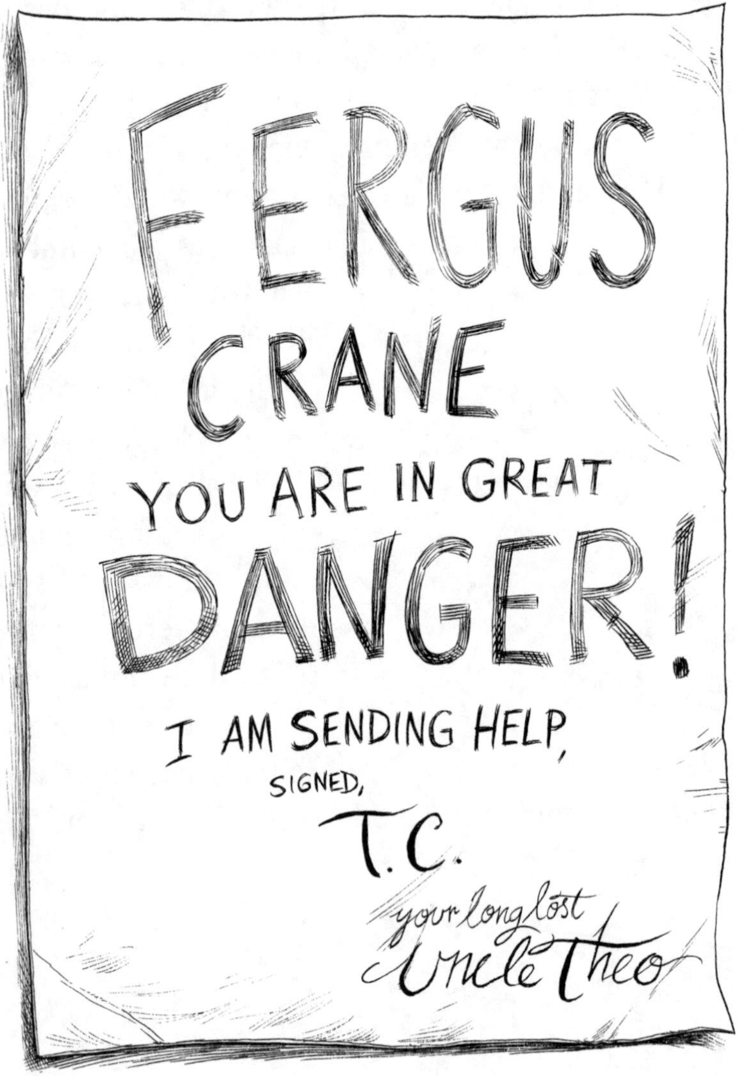
FERGUS
CRANE
YOU ARE IN GREAT
DANGER!
I AM SENDING HELP,
SIGNED,
T.C.
your long lost
Uncle Theo

Chapter Five

Peep-peep-peep! Peep-peep-peep! Peep-peep . . .
Fergus's eyes snapped open. It was seven
o'clock. He reached out and slammed his hand
down on the top of his alarm clock. The *peeping* stopped.

'I'll just have half a minute more in bed,' he whispered to himself. 'Half a minute . . .'

Half an *hour* later, he woke for a second time and
looked round the room groggily. Three nights of
staying up till midnight were beginning to take their
toll. He sat up, pushed the quilt away and stretched.
Then he caught sight of the mechanical box perched
above his head on the window ledge, its injured wing
trailing on one side.

He reached into his pyjama pocket and took out the

letter and read it again. He frowned. *Long-lost Uncle Theo*? His mother had never mentioned an Uncle Theo.

And what did he mean, *You are in great danger!*?

Danger from *what*? He certainly didn't feel in any great danger.

I am sending help.

Fergus wasn't sure he liked the sound of that. What sort of help? And what would his mother say?

Fergus glanced at the clock again. It was seven thirty-five. His mother would already be hard at work downstairs in the bakery. He would have to get a move on, otherwise he'd be late for school – and Captain Claw didn't take kindly to boys or girls who arrived late for school.

Fergus didn't want to spend the whole day half-way up the rigging, practising semaphore. Not again! Although the last time, he and Bolivia the parrot had ended up having quite a good time.

Springing into action, Fergus grabbed *Practical Potholing for Beginners*, stuffed it in his backpack and dashed downstairs. In the kitchen, he quickly devoured the breakfast croissant his mother had left out for him and snatched his lunchbox from the fridge. Back in the bathroom, he brushed his teeth. Then, swinging his backpack up onto his shoulders, he hurried from the apartment. The front door slammed behind him.

It was seven forty-three.

Fergus fairly flew down the stairs, skidding round at each landing before racing down the next flight. If Miss Jemima Gumm had emerged from her first-storey apartment a split second earlier, then she and her canaries – fluttering in the large cage on pram wheels – would have been sent flying. As it was, she was merely dragged along a couple of steps in Fergus's slipstream as he dashed past.

MISS JEMIMA GUMM

'Oh, Fergus,' she called, her voice as high and twittery as one of her beloved birds. 'Do thank your dear mother for the caraway seeds; so kind ...'

Her eyes darted back and forth behind her steel-rimmed spectacles. 'You haven't seen the Bigsby-Clutterbucks' cat, have you, dear? Dreadful creature!'

'No, Miss Gumm,' Fergus's voice floated back up the stairwell.

He reached the entrance hall and hurried across the cold marble tiles. Madame Lavinia and Arturo Squeegie were both checking their mail. Fergus skidded to a halt and

MADAME LAVINIA

tried to squeeze his way between them.

'Good morning, Mr Squeegie,' he said. 'Good morning Madame Lavinia.'

Madame Lavinia turned round, her large strings of amber beads clacking at her neck, her hair a haystack of frizzy orange, peppered with gold hairclips. 'Ah, Fergus! My little

ARTURO SQUEEGIE

maestro!' She laughed, a sound like the tinkling of an out-of-tune piano. 'What's the rush?'

'Late for school, old man?' Arturo Squeegie looked up from his letter box brandishing a lilac-scented letter, his jet black toupee glistening on his head. 'Oh, to be young again, eh, Madame Lavinia? Although in your case, lovely lady, you don't look a day over twenty-one.'

Arturo took Madame Lavinia's hand and gave it a theatrical kiss.

'Oh, Mr Squeegie!' laughed Madame Lavinia, the amber beads clacking noisily. 'You're too, too much, you really are!'

Fergus slipped past them.

'Have a good day,' trilled Madame Lavinia.

'Splice that mainbrace, old chap,' called Arturo Squeegie.

'Thank you!' Fergus called back. 'I shall.'

Reaching the door, Fergus opened it up and stepped out onto the street. It was seven fifty-one. Since he was setting off six minutes later than usual, he'd have to run extra fast.

As he raced past Beiderbecker's Bakery, Fergus

paused – as he did every day – to wave in through the window. Mrs Crane had been at work since five o'clock, and Fergus knew she liked to see him before he went to school – even if it was through the glass of a shop window. She looked up, a tired expression on her face, which vanished the moment she saw Fergus, to be replaced by a radiant smile. She gestured to his backpack and mouthed the words *lunch* and *box* exaggeratedly.

'Yes, yes, I've got my lunchbox,' Fergus muttered. He raised a thumb to show her he'd understood, and dashed off.

He sped past the cafes and shops, past Antonio the hurdy-gurdy man and the spot where Wall-eyed Ned paraded back and forwards in front of the

theatre. He dashed down a side alley, past the bagel stall and on down to the canal where he sprinted along the canal side.

As he rounded Cyclops Point, where the old harbour lighthouse stood, the sails and masts of the *Betty-Jeanne* came into view. Without easing up for a moment, Fergus dashed along the quayside and skidded to a halt at the gangplank. Beside it, a small signpost read *The School Ship Betty-Jeanne* in gold letters above a picture of a rather stern-looking mermaid in a mortar-board.

'Good morning! Good morning!' screeched a voice, and Fergus looked up to see Bolivia – Captain Claw's red and blue parrot – perched on the balustrade at the top of the plank. 'Look at the time! Look at the time!'

BOLIVIA

44

'I know,' said Fergus. He crossed the swaying gang-plank. 'Don't tell Captain Claw, Bolivia, or it'll be the rigging for me.'

'Waving flags! Waving flags!' said Bolivia, jumping from one foot to the other.

Fergus grinned. 'Yes, I know you like semaphore practice,' he said, 'but I know something you like even more!' He swung the backpack from his shoulders and pulled out his lunchbox.

'Florentines! Florentines!' Bolivia squawked excitedly.

'Yes, yes,' said Fergus. 'But keep it down. We don't want the whole school to hear.' Fergus looked at the lunchbox. 'What the . . ?'

It wasn't his old familiar lunchbox – which was actually an old Beiderbecker cake tin held shut with a piece of string. No, this lunchbox was brand new and shiny, with little buttons along its top, and small doors and

compartments. On one side, a small label said *"The Lunchomatic"; The Fateful Voyage Trading Co.*

In his rush to get to school, Fergus hadn't even looked at it. Now that he did, he could see that, as lunchboxes went, this was clearly an expensive one.

He pressed one of the buttons on the lid. A little door clicked open and a nutty, chocolatey, caramelly aroma wafted out. Bolivia clacked her beak.

'Florentines! Florentines!' she squawked. 'My favourite! My favourite!'

Fergus smiled. Ever since he had started at the school ship *Betty-Jeanne* two terms ago, Bolivia and he had been the best of friends – and all because of the cakes and pastries that Fergus's mother packed in his lunchbox. Sometimes he would give the parrot a little piece of croissant; sometimes some walnut eclair, or a corner of flapjack. Her absolute favourites, however, were *Archduke Ferdinand's Florentines*.

Fergus remembered his first day at school with a shudder. Although almost nine years old, he had never been to school before. His mother simply couldn't afford it, so she'd done her best to teach him at home, after work – and sometimes *at* work.

Fergus smiled. Writing stories at night and doing maths at the cake counter had been fun, and he'd loved the afternoons, exploring the neighbourhood and making friends with everyone.

But all that had changed when the *Betty-Jeanne* had sailed into the harbour and docked at the canal quayside. Fergus remembered how excited his mother had been when she read one of the bill posters that Captain Claw had stuck up all over town.

The School Ship Betty-Jeanne, it had said. *Offers all the benefits of a top class education, with the proven virtues of the nautical way of life absolutely free.*

The word 'free' was in extra large letters, with a picture

THE SCHOOL SHIP
BETTY-JEANNE

OFFERS ALL THE BENEFITS OF A **TOP CLASS** EDUCATION, WITH THE PROVEN **VIRTUES** OF THE NAUTICAL WAY OF LIFE ABSOLUTELY **FREE**

WE'RE LOOKING FOR YOUNG, ABLE-BODIED — **STUDENTS** —
CANDIDATES MUST BE AGILE, ATHLETIC, AND GOOD AT SQUEEZING THROUGH SMALL SPACES

EXTREMELY LIMITED NUMBER OF PLACES SO

APPLY NOW! TO CAPTAIN HORATIO SMOLLET HEADMASTER.

of the mermaid in a mortar-board pointing at it for added effect.

'Look, Fergus!' his mother had said. 'They're looking for young, able-bodied students . . . Must be agile, athletic, good at squeezing through small spaces . . . Oh, Fergus!' she'd cried. 'You're exactly what they're looking for. And just think, you'd get a top-class education, absolutely free!'

'But I already get an education absolutely free,' Fergus had mumbled. But when he had looked at his mother's face, her excitement giving way to a look of love and concern, he had known that her mind was made up.

So it was that, on the appointed afternoon, along with dozens of others, Fergus had gone along to the tall-masted clipper for an interview. Dressed in his smartest clothes and with his hair slicked down, he'd been asked questions by Captain Claw like, 'How tall are you, lad?' and 'Are you afraid of small spaces?', and been made to climb to the top of the rigging.

At the end of it all, the captain had turned to Mrs Crane and said, 'Congratulations, Madame. We'll make a scholar and a seaman out of your little treasure.'

Which is how Fergus had found himself - at the age of nearly nine, and never having been to school before in his life - walking up the gangplank on the first day of term, feeling very small and a little frightened, and making friends with a parrot.

Fergus glanced at his watch and groaned. It was eleven minutes past eight. He was already eleven minutes late for his first lesson; gym class with Mr Woodhead. He took the Florentine out of his strange new lunchbox and gave it to the parrot, who promptly flew up to the crow's nest - or as the children on the *Betty-Jeanne* called it, 'the parrot's nest' - at the top of the mast.

'*Twelve* minutes past,' Fergus groaned, checking his watch again. Any later, and he'd end up on barnacle-scraping duty . . .

Things were looking almost as bad as on that very first day on board the *Betty-Jeanne*. To start with, he'd had to meet his new classmates - or *ship*mates, as they were instructed to call each other. They were all lined up in a row on the foredeck.

There was big, beefy Horace Tucker, with his mass of unruly straw-like hair and spectacles held together

49

with sticky tape. Next to him was little Tessa Maas, smaller than Fergus, with a black bob and dark, serious eyes: the others soon nicknamed her 'Mouse'. Then there was Sylvie Smith, with her ginger plaits, long, freckled legs and knock-

HORACE TUCKER

TESSA MAAS "MOUSE"

knees. And finally, Jimmy 'Spike' Thompson, who was just a little taller than Fergus, but much stockier and twice as strong.

And that was it, the entire school. A mere handful of pupils. For, of all the many hopefuls who had applied to join the school ship *Betty-Jeanne*, Captain Claw had selected only five.

Certainly, they were a motley crew, Fergus had to admit, from all parts of town and with only one thing in common – none of them had parents who could afford to send them to either Montmorency

Academy or Harbour Heights. After that first awkward meeting, however, they'd soon become friends.

Horace was the class joker and clown. Mouse fussed over them all, and Spike was brave and fearless, and took it upon himself to protect Sylvie, who was the nervous, tearful type. And then there was Fergus; amiable, happy-go-lucky, a little short for his age perhaps, but excellent at getting on with people.

SYLVIE SMITH

JIMMY "SPIKE" THOMPSON

Yes, they were a motley crew all right – though they were nothing compared to the teachers aboard the *Betty-Jeanne*!

Fergus might never have been to school before, but he knew what teachers looked like. They looked like Dr Fassbinder. They wore old tweed jackets with leather patches at the elbows, they had long striped scarves from their university days, and were always losing their spectacles when in fact they were on a chain round their neck the whole time. But the teachers on board the *Betty-Jeanne* were nothing like Dr Fassbinder.

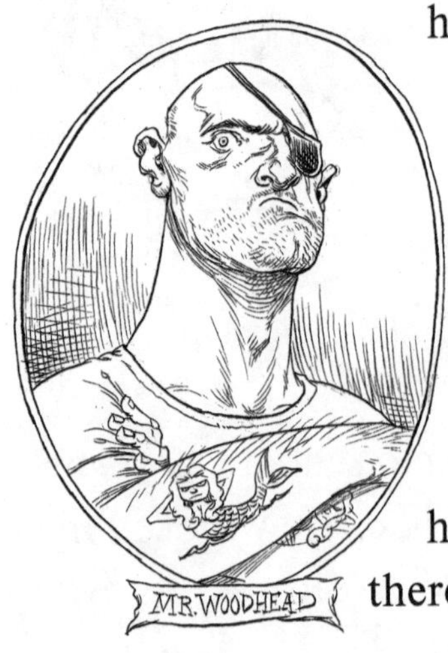

MR. SPICER

There was Mr Spicer, with his big hooped earrings and red

MRS. BLOOD

MR. WOODHEAD

beard. He was meant to teach geography, but all they ever seemed to study was caves and tunnels and 'potholing for beginners'. Then there was Mrs Blood the science teacher who liked gunpowder and cannons, and didn't seem to wash very much. And Mr Woodhead, who taught gym, with his eye-patch and tattoos of mermaids on his arms.

Fergus was pretty sure the mermaid in the mortar-board on the school sign had been copied from Mr Woodhead's right forearm.

MR. GILROY

And then, in his filthy apron, there was Mr Gilroy. He had a wooden leg carved like a table leg, with notches – twelve in all – down one side. He was the school cook, although as everyone brought lunchboxes, he only ever cooked for the teachers – which was just as well, judging by the smells coming out of the galley of the *Betty-Jeanne*.

But perhaps the strangest teacher of them all was Captain Claw himself.

CAPTAIN CLAW

Fergus hung his backpack up on his hook in the cloakcabin, and struggled into his gym kit. He checked his watch. Fourteen minutes past. He rushed across the foredeck, past the headmaster's cabin and . . .

'*Uurghh!*' he croaked as a hooked hand shot out from the open doorway and snagged the back of his vest.

Chapter Six

The next moment, Fergus found himself staring into the headmaster's angry red face.

'Crane!' he barked. 'I might have known. Late again!'

'It's . . . it's . . . only . . . b . . . been the once . . . s . . . s . . . sir,' stammered Fergus, dangling by the back of his vest from Captain Claw's clawlike hook.

'Don't bandy words with me, you lily-livered landlubber!' roared Captain Claw.

The headmaster of the school ship *Betty-Jeanne* liked calling the children 'landlubbers' and 'harbourhuggers' and 'scurvy dogs'. Fergus had no idea what these words meant, but he was sure they weren't good.

'Keelhauling's too good for you, you undersized

shark-bait!' he growled. 'I've half a mind to give you a day's semaphore practice, except you seemed to enjoy it last time!'

From up in the parrot's nest, there came a squawk. 'Captain Claw! Captain Claw!'

'That infernal bird!' thundered the headmaster, releasing Fergus and striding to the door. 'How many times do I have to tell you?' he shouted up at Bolivia. 'It's Headmaster Smollet, you squawking feather-duster!'

'Wind in the east! Wind in the east!' squawked the parrot.

Good old Bolivia, thought Fergus. Trying to distract the headmaster for me.

'Storm on the horizon! Storm on the horizon!'

'Nonsense,' said Captain Claw who, despite his best efforts, was called Captain Claw by all the children behind his back. 'I swear that bird is getting dafter by the day – not to mention plumper. Must cut down on its birdseed. Now, where's my telescope? Storm on the horizon indeed!'

'In the corner, sir,' said Fergus, trying to be helpful. 'On your sea-chest.'

North Harbour

The captain's cabin (or Headmaster's study, as he called it) was a jumble of oil lamps, tarpaulins, nautical instruments and

West port

rusty harpoons. On the walls were strange stuffed fish from faraway oceans, and old, faded photographs of exotically dressed ladies, each with the name of a port written beneath them in the captain's scrawly handwriting. 'North Harbour' looked as if she needed a shave, and 'West Port' had only one tooth in her smile. Fergus's favourite was 'Sweetwater Keys'. She

Sandy Cove

had a large flower behind each ear and wore a long grass skirt.

'Ah, yes,' said Captain Claw, picking up the telescope distractedly.

Sweet Water Keys

Bolivia's ruse had worked. The headmaster seemed to have forgotten why Fergus was standing in his study. He loomed over the boy, tapping the tip of the telescope against the brim of his peaked cap.

Behind him, on his desk, was an enormous sea chart, weighed down at each corner by a heavy orange and grey speckled stone. When he wasn't bellowing orders at the teachers or telling the children off, Captain Claw would spend hours in his cabin, poring over the map, his clawlike hook tracing lines across it as he muttered to himself.

'Very good, Crane,' the captain said at last, striding out of the cabin and across the foredeck, telescope half-raised to his eye. 'Dismissed!'

As he slipped from the cabin and the door swung shut behind him, Fergus let out a sigh of relief. He looked at his watch. It was twenty-nine minutes past eight. Mr Woodhead's gym lesson would be well underway in the school gym, which was actually the cargo hold of the *Betty-Jeanne*.

Heading back along the corridor, Fergus turned right, then right again onto a wooden staircase. He hurried below deck, down one rickety flight of stairs after the other, into the interior of the ship.

As he went past the staffroom, his nose crinkled up at the stale odour of smelly socks, mixed up with Mrs Blood's pipe-smoke and Mr Gilroy's pilchard stew. Down past the gun deck he continued, where Mrs Blood took the science class next to the old cannons and barrels of gunpowder. He turned left at the galley, holding his nose, and down a final ladder to the gym.

Fergus paused, pressed his ear to the double-doors, and listened closely. He couldn't hear anything. Perhaps gym was over, or better still, cancelled . . .

All at once, the doors slid open. Fergus tumbled inside and fell heavily to the floor. He looked up to see Mr Woodhead towering above him, his hands on his hips and a thin smile playing on his lips.

'Well, if it isn't Fergus Crane!' he said, his nasal voice rasping unpleasantly. 'So good of you to join us. Catching up on your beauty sleep perhaps?'

'I . . . I'm sorry, sir,' said Fergus.

'As you're on your belly already, Mister Crane,' sneered Mr Woodhead, his one good eye glinting malevolently, 'you can give me ten!' Fergus began to do push-ups while Mr Woodhead turned to the rest of the class, who were standing, red-faced and panting, behind him. 'And that goes for the rest of you fine ladies and gentlemen,' he barked. 'Give me ten!'

The class groaned and got down on the dusty floor.

'And when you've finished that,' Mr Woodhead shouted, 'it's everybody's favourite, the Tunnel Exercise!'

The class groaned again.

'And in honour of our latecomer this morning,' Mr Woodhead added nastily. 'We'll do it twice!'

Chapter Seven

'S tand by your tunnels!' bellowed Mr Woodhead. The class did as they were told. They were standing facing the four corners of the gym beside four trapdoors, each with a name chalked onto it. Horace stood next to a trapdoor marked *The Glory Hole*, Mouse was next to one called *The Big Dipper*, while Sylvie Smith, looking as if she was about to burst into tears, stood next to one called *The Corkscrew*. Spike Thompson shot her a reassuring look from his corner where he stood next to a trapdoor marked *The Devil's Pot*. Each one of them had a whistle on a ribbon round their neck.

Fergus stood in the middle of the gym looking miserable. Nobody liked the Tunnel Exercise, but

Fergus liked it least of all. That was because he was 'the Spare'. Fergus didn't like being 'the Spare', but

there was nothing he could do about it.

Mr Woodhead blew his whistle and the four children opened the trapdoors and crawled through them into the ship's ballast below.

Ballast, as Fergus now knew all too well, was the name given to the boulders, stones and rubble in the very depths of a vessel that weigh it down in the water and keep a ship with masts as tall and heavy as the *Betty-Jeanne*'s from toppling over.

In the Tunnel Exercise, the children had to crawl along their own individual tunnels through the ballast, each one of which came up in a different place in the ship.

The Big Dipper zigzagged up and down,

and was perfect for Mouse, who was nimble and quick-witted. It came out in the rope store. *The Corkscrew,*

which went in an awkward spiral to the fo'c'sle, was given to lithe, double-jointed Sylvie. *The Devil's Pot* – a particularly testing tunnel which needed all of Spike's strength and endurance to complete – emerged just below the anchor chain. As for *The Glory Hole*, this was Fergus's least favourite, as it came up in Mr Gilroy's galley, in the corner where he threw his old fish heads. Horace, who was best at holding his breath, was given this one to tackle.

Everyone was familiar with his or her own tunnel, since they did the Tunnel Exercise every day. But as 'the Spare', Fergus had to know all four tunnels equally well. It was a good thing he was especially good

at squeezing through very small places, he thought to himself, because . . .

A whistle sounded. It came from the trapdoor marked *The Corkscrew*.

'Not again!' said Mr Woodhead crossly. He nodded at Fergus. 'Do your job, Crane!'

Fergus jumped to it. He shot down *The Corkscrew* trapdoor and snaked round and round in the dark. He could feel the wooden struts that held the tunnel walls in place, although here and there, a loose pebble pattered onto his shoulders. Round the fourth bend he found Sylvie, who was weeping so much she could no longer blow her whistle.

'It's all right, Sylvie,' Fergus whispered. 'I'll get you out, don't worry.'

'I'm stuck, Fergus!' wailed Sylvie. 'I'm always getting stuck. I'm useless, pathetic. I'm always letting everyone down.'

'Relax,' said Fergus, crawling up behind her. 'You'll be fine. You're the best of all of us at the Tunnel Exercise when you put your mind to it, and as for *Practical Pot-holing for Beginners*, I bet you can recite the whole book by heart now.'

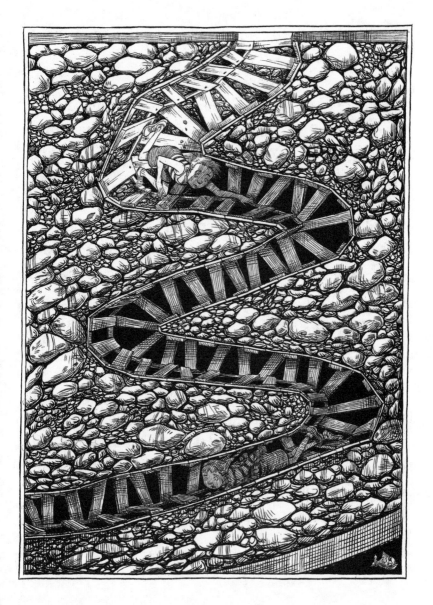

Sylvie smiled. 'It's my head, Fergus. I can't move it . . .'

'Look,' said Fergus, reaching out. 'Your plaits. They're snagged on this timber strut . . . There you go,' he announced a moment later as he tugged them free.

'Ouch!' yelped Sylvie, then smiled. 'Thank you, Fergus. You're so kind and brave.'

'Only doing my job,' said Fergus. 'Now hurry up. Woodenhead said we had to do this twice, remember!'

By the time they'd got to the fo'c'sle, turned round and come back, the others had already completed their second journeys.

'Come on, come on!' said Mr Woodhead testily as Sylvie and Fergus crawled out of *The Corkscrew* trapdoor. 'I should make you do it again five times.'

Sylvie looked ready to burst into tears again, and Spike stepped forward and put a hand on her shoulder.

'But luckily for you,' Mr Woodhead continued, giving him a nasty look, 'it's almost lunchtime, and goodness knows why, considering Short John's . . . I mean, Mr Gilroy's cooking, but I'm hungry. Class dismissed!'

Chapter Eight

The class gathered round the prow to eat their packed lunches as they always did. The foredeck was what passed for a playground on board the *Betty-Jeanne*. There was a rather wonky hopscotch game painted on the deck, and several barrels to sit on.

The carved prow of Betty-Jeanne herself stuck out in front of them. It was a painted figure of a plump lady with a rather ample bosom covered by two large scallop shells. Horace had nicknamed her 'the big mermaid'. Once, for a dare, he'd leaned over and painted a large curling moustache on her in the black tar meant for painting the *Betty-Jeanne*'s hull. The teachers had yet to notice.

BETTY-JEANNE

Right now, nobody was paying Betty-Jeanne any notice. Everyone was clustered round Fergus admiring his new lunchbox.

'Press that button again,' Mouse was saying.

Fergus pressed the button and a bottle shaped like a penguin popped up.

'Now try that one,' Spike joined in.

Fergus pressed the second button and a tray shot out that, a few minutes earlier, had contained cheese and tomato sandwiches, but now held nothing but a few crumbs. Fergus pushed it back in.

'*The Lunchomatic,*' read Sylvie Smith. '*The Fateful Voyage Trading Company.* What a curious name.'

'My mum does some part-time work for them,' said Fergus. 'They always seem to be sending parcels full of strange stuff.'

'Like what?' asked Mouse.

'Well,' said Fergus, 'last week they sent a batch of cocktail shakers with instructions that each one had to be shaken vigorously to check for rattles. And yesterday a parcel arrived full of paper horses and paper wings, with instructions on how to fit them together.'

'That sounds easy,' said Sylvie.

'That's what my mum thought,' said Fergus. 'And the best bit is that they pay in advance – and quite a lot, my mum said.'

'*My* mum could do with work like that,' said Spike. 'What's the address of this Fateful Voyage Trading Company?'

'I don't know,' said Fergus. 'And nor does my mum. She said that just after she baked that cake for Dr Fassbinder's faculty party – you know, the one with the icing-sugar penguins – and her picture appeared next to it in the *Montmorency Gazette* . . .'

Montmorency
Gazette

CYCLOPS

PINK PENGUINS BREAK THE ICE AT PROF'S PARTY

Beiderbecker's Bakery pulled out all the stops to produce a truly memorable finale to the Montmorency High School English Faculty party yesterday.

The sumptuous chocolate sponge gateau was topped with fondant icing and handcrafted icing sugar penguins. It was

Dr Fassbinder and the cake's creator, Lucia Crane

greeted by gasps of surprise when it was unveiled. Dr Fassbinder of the English Department told our reporter that the cake was "like a work of art . . . only tastier".

. . . continued on page 4

LAUGHING GOAT STATUE UNVEILED IN MONTMORENCY GARDENS

'Yes, I remember that!' said Sylvie excitedly.

'Well,' said Fergus, turning the lunchbox over in his hands, 'just after that, a card came offering my mum work. And soon after *that*, the parcels started arriving. When she's finished one, she leaves it at the Post Office in the harbour square, and another one arrives.'

'What does *this* one do?' said Horace, who'd been busy feeding his luncheon-meat sandwiches to the seagulls, but had just joined the others. He jabbed a finger at a small button on the underside of the box.

There was a loud click, followed by a short buzzing sound, and six stubby mechanical legs appeared along its sides. Everyone gasped, including Fergus, who jumped off the barrel he'd been sitting on with surprise. Before anyone could stop it, the lunchbox clattered onto the deck and scuttled off, past the hopscotch markings and towards Captain Claw's cabin.

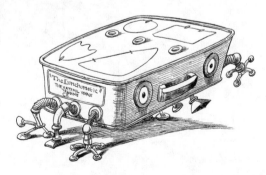

Just then, the bell rang for afternoon lessons. Mr Spicer appeared on the foredeck. 'Come along now, class,' he droned as he fiddled with one of his gold earrings. 'I hope you've all been studying your *Practical Pot-holing for Beginners*, because today we've got a test.'

'A test?' said Fergus as the rest of the class traipsed after Mr Spicer. 'Nobody told *me*.'

'Cool lunchbox, by the way,' said Horace, smiling. 'Hope you get it back.'

Chapter Nine

The classroom seemed stuffier than ever that afternoon and, following the morning's Tunnel Exercise, the entire class had trouble staying awake. Not that Mr Spicer seemed to notice. He just handed out the test papers and sat in his swivel chair, feet up on the desk, idly playing with the gold hoop in his left ear.

'No talking,' he said lazily, and began humming a tune from the new production of *The Cycling Fish* entitled 'Daisy's Lament'.

Fergus looked at the test paper.

How might one traverse a lateral tunnel, and how many easy steps might this take? Please number them clearly in your answer.

Fergus looked round at the rest of the class. Sylvie was writing furiously, already on her second sheet of paper. Horace was looking out of the window, smiling to himself. Spike and Mouse were both sucking their pencils, deep in thought. Perhaps it was because none of them had been able to go to school before now that they all, except maybe Horace, took their studies seriously. Nobody wanted to let their parents down.

Fergus sighed. The previous night, he'd only got to the second step in the book before nodding off. *'Secure your crampon to the rock face and proceed to the lip of the transverse tunnel . . .'* he remembered, but then what?

Fergus had absolutely no idea.

Instead of studying his copy of *Practical Pot-holing for Beginners*, he'd spent the whole evening waiting for a flying box from someone claiming to be his long-lost Uncle Theo. What had it said again? Oh, yes. *You are in great danger!*

'Danger of failing this test,' Fergus muttered unhappily.

I am sending help!

I could do with some help right now, thought

Fergus drowsily. His head began to nod, his eyes closed and . . .

'Time's up!' bellowed Mr Spicer. 'Class dismissed! Hand in your test papers on your way out.'

Fergus looked down at his paper. It was blank except for a thumb-mark and an ink blot resembling a fat rabbit. He handed it in anyway and hurried to the cloakcabin, where the others were picking up their bags and saying their goodbyes. Fergus went to his hook and stopped in surprise.

'Look at that!' said Horace over his shoulder. 'Fergus's lunchbox has climbed back into his backpack. How cool is that?'

Calling his goodbyes, Fergus headed down the gangplank and was just about to head off along the canal side, when Bolivia swooped down and fluttered, screeching, inches above his head.

'Don't come to school tomorrow! Don't come to school tomorrow!'

'News travels fast,' said Fergus bitterly. 'So you've heard about my test paper already. Don't worry, Bolivia.' He waved the parrot away. 'I promise I'll do better tomorrow!'

Chapter Ten

hat with the Tunnel Exercise and the previous night's lack of sleep, Fergus was exhausted. The walk home took him nearly twice as long as usual.

He turned left at the statue of General Montmorency and trudged through the narrow alleys. Turning right, he pushed past a queue of schoolgirls from Harbour Heights clustered round Old Mother Bleeny's bagel-stand, giggling and gossiping excitedly, and walked slowly along Boulevard Archduke Ferdinand.

'Afternoon, Fergus,' Ned the sandwich-board man called out.

Fergus trudged past in a daze. Further along the

road, he didn't seem to hear the mournful music of Antonio the hurdy-gurdy man, and he completely ignored Pepe the monkey when it held out its tasselled fez to him.

Past the familiar shops he went, head down. *Madame Aimee's Wedding Gowns. H.H. Luscombe's Umbrellas. Le Café Rondel. Joshua Berwick: Bespoke Tailor* . . . He didn't acknowledge a single nod or wave.

Arriving at the front door of Archduke Ferdinand Apartments, Fergus fumbled for his keys and let himself in. As he reached the first landing he could see Major and Mrs Bigsby-Clutterbuck waving their arms about and talking loudly, while Miss Jemima Gumm stood beside them in a pair of worn-looking carpet slippers, weeping loudly and pointing at the carved lintel above her front door.

'Do get him down, Barty!' Mrs Bigsby-Clutterbuck was shouting. 'No! No! Not like that! You're frightening him!'

MR & MRS BIGSBY-CLUTTERBUCK

PRINCE CASPIAN

'I'm doing my best, Maudie!' bellowed the major. 'If you could just quieten poor Miss Gumm down, perhaps I could hear myself think!'

'Horrid cat! Horrid, horrid cat!' Miss Gumm was wailing. 'Look, look! It's got a poor little blackbird in its mouth. Oooh!' she wailed even louder. 'I can't bear it!'

Fergus looked up. There, perched on the carved head of Archduke Ferdinand which graced the impressive lintel above Miss Gumm's front door, crouched Prince Caspian, the Bigsby-Clutterbuck's Persian cat, something black clasped firmly in its mouth.

'Cassie, Cassie baby.' Mrs Bigsby-Clutterbuck's voice was thick and honeyed. 'Come to Mummy, there's a good boy. You don't want to hurt the little birdie-wirdie, now do you?'

'Poor little bird!' wailed Miss Gumm.

Just then, two heads appeared over the stairwell above. 'Is everything all right down there?' called Madame Lavinia.

'I'm running a little late, but if I can be of any assistance,' Dr Fassbinder added, following her down the stairs.

'It's Prince Caspian.' Major Bigsby-Clutterbuck cleared his throat and assumed a military bearing. 'Been out on a recce. Come back with a little something. Ran up Miss Gumm's door frame. Won't come down. Cats will be cats.'

'Poor little bird!' wailed Miss Gumm for a second time.

'Quite a little show we've got down here,' came a deep musical voice from the second floor.

All eyes turned to the stairway.

'Hello, everybody!' Eugenie Beecham was making her entrance.

She was dressed in a shimmering fishscale dress of iridescent green, topped off with a stunning coral tiara that sparkled with sequins. In one hand she carried a long trident; in the other, a bicycle pump. She fluttered her long beautiful eyelashes. For a moment there was complete silence in the chilly hallway.

'What's everybody staring at?' Eugenie asked. 'Oh, this?' she said, patting her shimmering dress and

giving a little tinkling laugh. 'This is my costume.'

'Costume?' said Dr Fassbinder and Madame Lavinia at the same time.

'Yes, my costume. I'm having a fitting. They haven't got it quite right yet.' She paused. 'I'm "Daisy" in *The Cycling Fish*.'

'Of course, of course,' said Dr Fassbinder, blushing. 'I was going to see it the other night, but I seemed to have mislaid my tickets.'

'Fergus! *Daaarling!*' trilled Eugenie, sweeping past everyone on the landing and descending on Fergus. 'How's my little sailor? Why the glum face?'

'I don't want to talk about it,' said Fergus quietly.

'Let Eugenie cheer you up!' she continued, throwing her head back and bursting into song. *'Ohhh! Sweet Alfred, my heart is breaking . . .'*

As she hit the high note in 'breaking', Prince Caspian gave a squeal of alarm, dropping its catch as it leaped from the Archduke's head onto the marble floor, and scrambled through the Bigsby-Clutterbuck's open door. Everyone gathered round the little black body lying on the cold floor.

'It's . . . it's . . .' trembled Miss Gumm.

'MY TOUPEE!' shrieked Arturo Squeegie, dashing down the stairs from the second floor, his silk dressing gown flapping – and his bald head gleaming.

Fergus left them singing and arguing and laughing and crying. It really had been an exhausting day. He climbed slowly to the fourth floor, took out his key and opened the little front door.

'Home at last,' he sighed, slipping off his backpack.

'Is that you, Fergus?' Mrs Crane's voice floated out of the sitting room. 'Good day at school?'

'Fine,' Fergus called back, untruthfully. He popped his head round the sitting-room door. 'But I'm tired. I'm going to my room.'

Mrs Crane was sitting on a cushion, a box in front of her with a label on its side which read *The Fateful Voyage Trading Co.*, and a form in her hand. She looked up.

'Before you go, dear, you've got to help me with this,' she said. 'It's my latest job. It arrived this morning.'

'What is it?' said Fergus, giving a big yawn.

'Your new lunchbox, Fergus.' His mother laughed.

'You were testing it for me, or rather, for the Fateful Voyage Trading Company. And all you have to do is answer these simple questions.'

Dear Valued Worker,

Please read the following and answer the questions as honestly as you can.

Thanking you in anticipation, and with very best wishes

Fergus sat down on a cushion next to his mother and looked at the form.

Dear Valued Worker, it read. *Please read the following and answer the questions as honestly as you can.*

Thanking you in anticipation, and with very best wishes, Finn, Bill and Jackson, Vice-Presidents, The Fateful Voyage Trading Co.

'Number one,' read his mother. 'Did the *Lunchomatic* keep your lunch fresh?'

'I suppose so,' yawned Fergus.

'Number two. Did the *Lunchomatic* keep your lunch safe and undamaged?'

'Yes,' said Fergus.

His mother put another tick in the box provided. 'Number three . . .'

'How much longer?' moaned Fergus.

'This is the last question, dear,' said his mother patiently. 'Did the *Lunchomatic* live up to your hopes and expectations?'

'Well, it sprouted six legs and ran around when you pressed a button if that's what you mean. And my friend Horace told me it was well cool!' said Fergus, getting up.

'I'll put "yes" then,' said his mother.

She looked at Fergus, a look of concern in her eyes. 'You *are* looking tired,' she said. 'Maybe you're coming down with something. Perhaps you shouldn't go to school tomorrow.'

Fergus smiled. 'That's the second time someone's said that to me today,' he said, and went to his room, where he flung himself onto his bed and promptly fell fast asleep.

Chapter Eleven

ergus awoke with a start. A large shiny beetle with gleaming eyes was sitting on his chest. He froze in horror. He must be having a nightmare. Strange markings on the insect's sides glowed faintly in the dark.

The Lunchomatic, he read. *The Fateful Voyage Trading Co.*

Fergus gave a sigh of relief.

'Get off me, you stupid thing!' he said, brushing the lunchbox off.

It clattered to the floor, then scuttled to the window and clambered onto the sill, where it perched, its buttons glowing a deep orange.

'What is it *now*?' said Fergus irritably, throwing off

his quilt and padding over to the window.

Outside, the clock in Montmorency Gardens struck twelve.

Clouds that had been gathering earlier in the evening had cleared once more, and the full moon was shining brightly now, turning everything below it to burnished silver. Fergus looked down. Beside him on the window sill was the little mechanical box with the injured wing. Fergus gently picked it up and put it in his pocket. All at once, the *Lunchomatic* began clicking excitedly.

And then Fergus saw it! His jaw dropped.

It was a huge creature in flight, with great silvery wings beating silently as it swooped down from the tops of the mountains to his left. At first Fergus thought it must be some kind of giant albatross, or swan – or perhaps a massive albino bat . . . Yet as it came closer, he saw that it was not a bird, nor any other living creature . . .

'But it can't be,' Fergus murmured, as he stared unblinking. 'It's not possible.'

As if in response, the great metal creature flapped its bolted wings, reared up and trampled at the air with its glinting hoofs. Fergus gasped with amazement.

'A flying horse,' he said, his voice quavering. 'A *mechanical* flying horse.'

You are in great danger! Uncle Theo's note had said. *I am sending help!*

The winged horse swooped down low over Archduke Ferdinand Apartments, and for a moment Fergus lost sight of it. He peered over the sill of the window as far as he dared. Just then, a huge metal face with a long, shiny snout and bright ball-bearing eyes loomed up in front of his own. Fergus's heart missed a beat.

'H . . . have you come for me?' he asked.

The horse gave no reply, but hovered in front of Fergus's window, its great wings beating in the same curious up-down circular movement as the little mechanical box.

'Do you want me to go with you?' he asked.

Beside Fergus, the *Lunchomatic* seemed in no doubt. It clambered to the edge of the sill and jumped onto the horse's back.

'Oh, well,' said Fergus doubtfully. Goodness knows

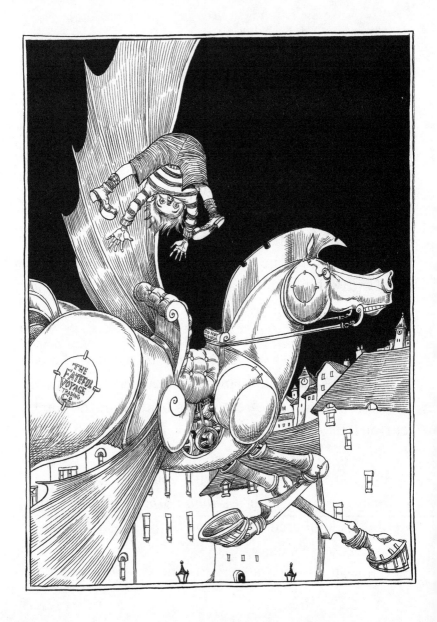

what his mother would say. 'Here goes,' he whispered as he inched his way along the window sill.

The chill wind whistled through the shutters. Beneath him – as he carefully manoeuvred himself to the very edge of the sill, his feet dangling into nothingness – the street lights seemed to telescope away.

'Don't look down,' he told himself.

He reached out with one hand and touched the cold metal of the creature's neck. All at once, the great winged horse lunged forwards, knocking him from the sill with one broad wing tip and catching him on its back. Fergus sat back in the padded saddle, the wind knocked out of him, struggling to catch his breath.

'Whoooaaaaa!' he cried out a moment later. It was all he could manage as Boulevard Archduke Ferdinand, Montmorency Gardens and the canal swept by in a smudge of muted shadow and light.

Pulling himself forward, Fergus was about to seize the reins when he noticed the label attached to them. *DO NOT TOUCH,* it said in big red letters. Instead, Fergus gripped the ornate pommel of the saddle and held on tightly.

Once around the harbour they flew, with the horse's huge wings beating effortlessly and the wind tugging at Fergus's clothes and ruffling his hair. Having got over the initial shock, Fergus was beginning to enjoy the flight.

'You are incredible,' he gasped, and patted the horse's shiny metal neck. 'Absolutely incredible!'

With a toss of its head and a beat of its wings, the great mechanical flying horse circled the old lighthouse at Cyclops Point, then soared off high into the

sky. Fergus leaned forward and clung on tightly round the horse's neck as the slumbering city fell away beneath him.

With his heart thumping and his stomach churning, he didn't know what he felt. Was he excited? Was he scared? As the snowy peaks of the mountains came closer, only one thing was certain.

Fergus Crane had just set out on the greatest adventure of his life!

Chapter Twelve

igher and higher they climbed. The mountains came closer. Fergus glanced back at the city – now little more than a patch of twinkling lights on the leeside of a stretch of jutting coastline. He felt giddy, light-headed and, as the winged horse continued to rise, the tips of his ears began to sting with cold. He turned and faced the front once more, and saw that the snow-covered mountain peaks were just before him.

Feeling a nudge in the small of his back, Fergus turned to find the *Lunchomatic* beeping insistently behind him. A small compartment opened and a scarf unfurled.

'Thank you,' said Fergus, taking it and wrapping it tightly round his ears.

Buoyed up by the rising currents of warm air, the flying horse tilted its wings and soared up over the mountains. Fergus looked down at the rugged snow-scape below him – jagged peaks and deep craters, snowy slopes and frozen lakes, all rushing past in a silvery blur.

Beyond the mountains, the land levelled out into a broad plateau, with fields and meadows and orchards, and narrow, fast-running rivers that cut through the fertile farmland. Beyond this was a forest, a vast dark expanse of angular pine trees, stretching off towards the horizon. And beyond the forest, the land abruptly fell away to a crinkled coastline and Fergus found himself flying far above a sprinkling of yellow islands, dotted like stepping-stones across a sparkling sea.

A sprawling city came next. Then more farmland; and a lake, set in the clearing of a great wood. And another coastline. And another. Then more islands, and yet more farmland, which gave way to a great barren wasteland of stunted shrubs and shifting sand . . .

And *still* the winged horse flew on.

Far ahead, Fergus could make out the looming shape of a distant range of mountains, its snowy jagged peaks pink and lemon in the light of the early morning sun . . .

'Early morning?' Fergus exclaimed. 'Have I really been flying so long?'

As they continued, and the patchwork landscape below went through more changes, Fergus realized that, for the first time since they had left the Archduke Ferdinand Apartments, the great mechanical winged horse was coming down lower in the sky. The scene beneath him grew larger, clearer.

There were terraced meadows, filled with long grass and pink, yellow, white and blue flowers, and big brown cows, wearing bells on collars around their necks; bells that Fergus could hear softly clanking. There were grape vines and peach trees, and a crystal clear stream that trickled down over dark grey rocks. Still lower they flew, skimming over a little wood, with oaks and ashes, silvery birches and coppery beeches . . .

Behind it was a garden, with a pond and a dove-cote. The ground came closer. There were clumps of pampas grass; goats and chickens; a croquet lawn . . . And there, sheltering in the lee of a tall, rocky outcrop, stood a magnificent mountain chalet.

The flying horse flapped its wings powerfully up and down and readied itself for landing. Fergus braced himself. The next moment, there was a soft bump as the horse came down lightly on the front lawn next to a bright yellow croquet hoop.

'Thank you,' said Fergus, patting the metal creature on the neck as he dismounted. In the clear light of the mountain morning, he noticed a plaque on the horse's side.

The Fateful Voyage Trading Co., it said.

Fergus stepped forward and looked up at the chalet. It was a large building, set upon stilts, with shingle tiles, a broad veranda and shutters decorated with hearts. There were logs stacked beneath the house and bales of hay in the open lofts at the top; there were window-boxes overflowing with hanging plants and flowers, while the doorway was festooned with an arch of tangled jasmine and climbing-roses. As he approached the door, Fergus noticed another plaque, on the wall beside a bell-pull. *The Fateful Voyage Trading Co.*; in silver letters.

Fergus seized the bell-pull and gave it a sharp tug. A clanking – not unlike the cow-bells – echoed round inside. The next moment he heard the sound of foot-steps approaching and a latch being lifted. The door swung open and Fergus found himself staring down at a dapper black and white penguin.

'I . . . *errm* . . . I'm looking for Mr Theo Crane,' he said uncertainly.

The penguin bowed politely, extended a flipper and beckoned. Fergus stepped inside and the penguin shut the door behind him.

Fergus shook his head, hardly able to take in what

he was seeing. He was standing in a long hallway, brightly lit and buzzing with activity – for everything there seemed to be moving.

The penguin beckoned a second time.

The wall-lights, Fergus realized, were shifting round constantly on angled brackets, sending their beams of light darting round the hallway like gleaming sabres. And there was a tall cabinet . . . Walking! Perhaps it was needed elsewhere; perhaps it was simply fed up with standing in the same place – either way, it had picked itself up and was clomping down the corridor. It passed an elegant bookcase, which was busily rearranging its shelves.

The penguin tapped its flipper against Fergus's leg. But Fergus didn't notice.

Mouth open, he was watching the chains above his head, constantly on the move, and wondering what was inside the knobbly packages

 that hung from the hooks attached to them.

The penguin tapped his leg a second time. Just then, a door to Fergus's left flew open and an angular contraption on squeaky wheels burst out and clattered along one of the networks of narrow tracks that criss-crossed the wooden floor. It disappeared into a second room, down the corridor on the right. Two more contraptions appeared and, navigating the tracks, sped away in opposite directions – to be replaced by half a dozen more.

Some were tall and spindly. Some were round and squat. Some were carrying things – everything from boxes of springs to reels of hosepipe; some were covered in instruments and dials; some seemed to serve no purpose whatsoever . . .

'If you don't mind,' said the penguin. 'This way, please.'

Fergus jumped. 'You can talk!' he spluttered.

The penguin was standing crossly, with its flippers

THEOSOPHUS CRANE

MARIANNA CRANE

NANNY & PATTY DUBOIS

on its hips and its head tilted. 'Of course I can talk,' it said. 'Parrots can talk, can't they? And penguins are far cleverer than parrots!'

'I suppose so,' said Fergus sheepishly. 'Sorry.'

The penguin nodded, beckoned again – exaggeratedly slowly – and waddled off across the hall and down a long corridor. Fergus followed. A few moments later, they came to a wide door. Ushering him forward with flapping flippers, the penguin bustled Fergus into the room.

Inside, Fergus found himself in a long gallery, with ornately framed paintings on one side of its panelled walls, and large windows on the other. Apart from the paintings, the gallery was unfurnished but for a leather armchair and a side table at the far end.

POLLY MOLLY & DOLLY
C.RANE

THE CRANE FAMILY

On the table lay a large leather book.

The door clicked shut behind him, and Fergus found himself alone.

So, he thought, his Uncle Theo worked for the Fateful Voyage Trading Company. And this place in the mountains must be its headquarters.

He turned away from the window and began to walk along the gallery, looking at the paintings that lined the wall opposite. They were all portraits – family portraits by the look of it. There was a painting of a stern-looking man in a tall top hat and winged collar; beneath it, the words, *Theosophus Crane*. Next to that was a kindly-faced old lady in a black lace cape, *Marianna Crane*, then a double portrait of a jolly couple called *Nanny and Pappy Dubois*. Fergus smiled. The next portrait was of three sisters; *Polly, Molly and Dolly Crane*, and after that came another group portrait . . .

Fergus stopped in his tracks.

The painting was of a father and mother and two sons. The older boy was about twelve, the younger . . . Fergus swallowed hard. The younger boy looked exactly like him! He read the plaque on the picture frame. *The Crane Family*, it said.

Fergus needed to sit down. He felt light-headed, and there was a strange fluttery feeling in his tummy. He went over to the armchair and flopped down heavily into the soft, leather upholstery. It was then that his eyes fell on the cover of the battered leather book on the table beside him.

The Log of the Betty-Jeanne, it said.

Chapter Thirteen

 ith a trembling hand, Fergus opened *The Log of the Betty-Jeanne* and began to read.

Ship's company

Captain	Marcus Crane
First Officer	Horatio Smollet
Cannoneer	Lizzie Blood
Seaman 1st class	Tom Spicer
Seaman 2nd class	Jack Woodhead
Cook	John Gilroy

Voyage to the Emerald Sea.

Day One

We set off on our voyage for the far-off Emerald sea with a fair wind and stout hearts. I have taken on a good crew for this trip I believe, though they are a little rough round the edges.

Bade farewell to my dear Lucia on the quayside, and my faithful brother, Theo. After the triumph of my last voyage to Magnet Island I have great hopes for this, my return to the Scorpion Archipelago. Have left Finn, Bill and Jackson with much regret, but Theo will have need of their help in the macadacchio business whilst I'm gone.

Day Two
A fair day's sailing. Little to report.

Day Three
Passed the Three Sisters, and sailed on into open waters.

Day Four
Had to speak firmly to Smollet about standards of behaviour. Gilroy's cooking leaves much to be desired.

Day Five
Felt unwell. Pilchard stew disagrees with me.

Day Six
Little to report.

Day Seven
Rough seas! Hard sailing. Had to reprim and Spicer for laziness and Woodhead for insolence...

The crested Puffin.

The Pink-eyed Whelk picker.

The Three Sisters.

Day Fourteen

Have spent the last week in bed, most unwell. Have decided to prepare my own meals from now on. Smollet has been in charge of my chart during my illness. I am afraid he is an indifferent navigator, prone to many errors. Now I am back on my feet, I have taken sole charge of plotting our course, and have corrected his mistakes.

Day Fifteen

We are becalmed. Smollet's errors were greater than I first realized, and we have strayed into that area of ocean all sea farers dread, "the Drifts". I fear the crew blame me for this misfortune. Am feeling much stronger today.

First Officer Smollet's Parrot.

Black-eyed Albatross.

Day Twenty-Four

Rations are running low and the crew becoming more insolent by the day. Am beginning to regret the rash way I hired them. Theo's words of warning might prove all too true. And poor Lucia begged me not to depart on this fateful voyage!

Day Thirty

Still becalmed. Rations almost gone.

Day Forty-One

Fortune has indeed smiled upon us! Two days ago the wind picked up and soon we had a full set of sails speeding us towards the Stormy Straits. Hard sailing, but all of us were desperate to strike land as our rations are completely exhausted. Smollet even contemplated eating his parrot three days ago. Poor thing took refuge in the crow's nest and refuses to come down even now.

This evening, we made landfall at Horse shoe Island. We have made it to the Emerald Sea! Spirits are high, but, as I took time to warn the crew, these are hazardous waters and our adventures are far from over.

Horse shoe Island.

Pyjama fish.

Warty Reef Eel.

Sand fish.

Spiky fish.

Big-Clawed Crab

Reef Oyster.

Day Forty-Six Set sail again, despite much grumbling from the crew. Horseshoe Island is indeed a comfortable haven with its white sandy beaches fringed with palm trees and multi-coloured coral teeming with fish and reef oysters. Had to reprimand Blood for firing the ship's cannon at the palm trees, "in order to collect coconuts" - or so she claimed. We hadn't voyaged this far for coconuts, I told her. We must save our powder for the sterner test to come.

<u>Day Fifty-One</u> We laid anchor at Magnet Island and I rowed ashore with Smollet and Woodhead. It was good to set foot on its golden sands and see the groves of mighty macadacchio trees again. As I wandered through them gathering the fallen macadacchio nuts, I quite forgot myself. After all, I owe my fortune to this remarkable nut – and, of course, to dear Theo's skills in the greenhouse. Without the few specimens I brought back from that first voyage, there would be no thriving Macadacchio business back home, and certainly not enough money to finance this latest voyage...

I couldn't resist tasting one and, as I bit into it, I thought of dear Lucia and her delicious Florentines waiting for me back home. I quite lost track of the time and missed Smollet and Woodhead, who had returned in the boat to the ship. I had to swim back, but the exercise did me good. Funny thing was, I arrived to find that the Betty-Jeanne was about to slip anchor without me. The crew all swear this was just an unfortunate mistake.

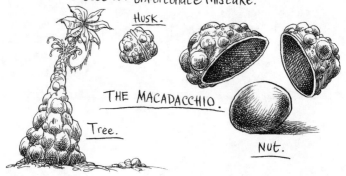

HUSK.

THE MACADACCHIO.

Tree.

NUT.

<u>Day Fifty-Two</u> Set sail for the furthermost island in the Scorpion Archipelago, Fire Isle, the purpose of our whole expedition.

I gathered the crew together on the fore deck and explained the reason we had sailed so far, and were about to enter even more perilous waters. Fire diamonds. To my surprise, they seemed to know all about them, claiming the fabled gems were common gossip in the harbour taverns.

Unfortunately they seemed rather crestfallen when I explained that, contrary to what they might have heard back home, the fire diamonds of Fire Isle don't just lie at the base of the volcano waiting to be picked up from the black sand. And their consternation grew when I told them that the indescribably precious stones are to be found only in the fire caverns deep inside the volcano itself, accessible only to the most agile and determined explorer. Smollet, in particular, swore the most bloodcurdling oaths and stomped about the foredeck, smashing into the gunnels with that infernal claw of his.

The atmosphere brightened when I revealed dear Theo's brilliant invention: the marvellous "Scuttle-Bug". I gave them a demonstration, winding the little fellow up, and setting it scuttling across the deck on its six little legs to pick up the coconuts I'd set up in the fo'c'sle. By the end, all were cheering, even Smollet.

SIDE.

TOP.

The Scuttle-Bug.

<u>Day Fifty-Four</u> As we approached Fire Isle, we could hear the volcano at its centre rumbling ominously. Black smoke billowed from its top and the sea round the island was dark and choppy. I quickly realised that we had arrived not a moment too soon and must go ashore immediately if we were to try for the fire diamonds, as the volcano was ready to erupt at any moment.

Smollet and the crew suddenly got cold feet at the sight of the monstrous smoking brute and wanted to know why we couldn't wait until after an eruption. I explained that if they didn't mind waiting nine years for the island to cool down, they could do precisely that. Smollet shot me a black look and cursed under his breath. I asked for volunteers, but all were too scared to accompany me.

I am most disappointed, but shall not be thwarted. Much to my irritation I cannot find my chart anywhere, but I shall just have to get along without it. I intend to take the scuttle-bug and row ashore without delay.

I finish this entry in the full knowledge that it may be my last, and if it is to be so, I have asked Smollet to make sure this log reaches my dear brother Theo, my good friends and comrades, Finn, Bill and Jackson, and my dear, darling wife Lucia,

SIGNED

Captain Marcus Crane

Too stunned to speak, Fergus turned the page. But there was nothing more. He sat in the armchair gazing out of the gallery windows at the mountains, trying to take it all in. The next moment, the door opened and three penguins marched in followed by a man in a mechanical walking chair.

'My dear Fergus,' he said. 'We meet at last. It's me, dear boy. Your long-lost Uncle Theo!'

he penguins were holding trayfuls of delicious breakfast things, and behind them walked a mechanical table set with places for two.

'Come, my boy,' said Uncle Theo, smiling kindly. 'Let's talk over breakfast. I'm sure you're hungry after your little trip, and I expect you have a few questions you'd like to ask.'

'I don't know where to begin,' said Fergus distractedly as the table settled in front of him and the penguins started setting down croissants, and hot chocolate, and pots of jam and honey on the white tablecloth.

'First things first,' said Uncle Theo, steering his chair over to join him. 'Meet Finn, Bill and Jackson, my associates. Jackson let you in on your arrival, I believe.'

UNCLE THEO

FINN, BILL & JACKSON

The penguins gave a little bow.

'If you'll excuse us,' said Finn, or perhaps Bill, or Jackson – Fergus wasn't sure which, 'we've got some pruning to do in the greenhouses.'

'Of course, Bill,' said Theo, pouring Fergus a large mug of foaming hot chocolate. 'You run along. Fergus and I have everything we need, don't we Fergus, my boy?'

'Yes,' said Fergus, taking the mug from his uncle and sipping it tentatively. It tasted delicious.

'Just a little something we're experimenting with here at the Fateful Voyage Trading Company,' Uncle Theo said as the penguins left the gallery. 'Hot chocolate with macadacchio nut essence . . .' He sighed, long and deep. 'Aah, the macadacchio nut! Where would the Cranes be without it? Why, that little nut has made all this possible.'

Uncle Theo spread his arms wide in a gesture that took in the whole gallery.

'But I'm getting ahead of myself,' he said, taking a croissant and giving it a liberal coating of honey. 'Fergus, you must have some questions. Ask away, old boy. Ask away.'

'How did you find me?' asked Fergus, a chocolatey moustache on his upper lip. 'And why are you my *long-lost* Uncle Theo? And why am I in danger? Danger from what? And . . .'

'Fergus, Fergus, Fergus,' smiled Uncle Theo, croissant crumbs round his mouth and his eyes twinkling behind his wire-framed spectacles. 'Relax, my dear boy, and have one of these excellent croissants. I shall tell you everything. But first, meet your family.'

He gestured to the portraits on the wall.

'That stern-looking gentleman in the top hat is my grandfather, your *great*-grandfather. He founded the family firm of Crane and Sons. Back then, we

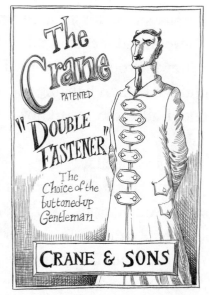

specialized in button-making. I take it you've heard of the "Crane Double Fastener"?'

Fergus shook his head.

'Never mind, never mind,' said Uncle Theo. 'Once, every raincoat worth the name had to have a "Crane Double Fastener". Next to him is grandmother Marianna, his wife, and there,' he said, pointing to the portrait of the jolly couple, 'are Nanny and Pappy Dubois, bless them. My mother's parents. My mother, your grandmother, was none other than the famous portraitist, Rachel Dubois. You must have heard of her.'

Fergus shook his head again.

'Never mind, never mind,' said Uncle Theo. 'Once, no drawing-room in the land was worth the name without a Dubois hanging above the mantelpiece. She painted all these, you know. Rather fine, don't you think?'

Fergus nodded.

'Next,' Uncle Theo continued, 'are my father's sisters. Aunts Polly, Molly and Dolly. Inseparable they were, right up to the very end.'

'The very end?' said Fergus.

'Terrible incident,' said Uncle Theo. 'During the second act of a production of the musical farce *The Cycling Fish*, the elephant escaped and ran amok in the stalls. They didn't stand a chance.'

'I've heard of *The Cycling Fish*!' said Fergus.

'Really?' said Uncle Theo surprised. 'I didn't think they performed it any more. How very curious . . . Anyway.' He cleared his throat. 'Here,' he said, and gestured to the family portrait on the wall above them, 'is my father, Theodore, my mother, Rachel, me and . . .'

'My father!' said Fergus excitedly.

'Indeed, indeed,' said Uncle Theo, a sad, faraway look in his eyes. 'Your father, the great Captain Marcus Crane, explorer and adventurer – and discoverer of the macadacchio nut!'

Fergus stared at the boy in the picture. The look on his face was the same image of cheeky-grinned, sparkly-eyed mischief that he knew so well from the photograph of his father at home.

'Dear Marcus,' Uncle Theo was saying. 'Back when my mother painted this, Crane and Sons had fallen on hard times. The "double fastener" was old-fashioned; everybody wanted zips, and we lived on the money my mother made from her painting. I remember Marcus saying to me when I was recovering from my illness . . .'

'Your illness?' said Fergus, turning back from the portrait.

'Rheumatic fever,' said Uncle Theo. 'After which, these . . .' He tapped his legs. 'Were quite, quite useless . . .'

His voice trailed away, and for a moment they sat in silence.

'Anyway, as I was telling you,' Uncle Theo continued, 'I remember Marcus saying to me, "Theo, there has to be more to life than buttons. There's a great big world out there, and you and I are going to explore it, together!" He was trying to cheer me up, you see,' Uncle Theo smiled. 'Both of us knew I'd never walk again, and that he'd have to do all the exploring on his own.

'After Papa died, I took over Crane and Sons, and Marcus set off on his first big adventure. The voyage to the Palace of Ice. That's where he met Finn, Bill and Jackson. Saved his life they did, rescuing him from the icemen on their walrus chariots - but that's a long

story. Remind me to tell you it some time.'

'I will,' said Fergus, his eyes wide with wonder.

'Well anyway, while Marcus was away, I moved out of buttons and into inventing. Oh, simple things at first – the Crane self-adjusting wall lamp; the automatic bookcase . . . I found I had a talent for it. All those years spent in bed and in wheelchairs had given me plenty of time to think, you see.'

Fergus nodded, helping himself to another croissant.

'Crane and Sons was just about keeping its head above water, and I even managed to find the money to buy an old tea-clipper for Marcus's next voyage.'

'The *Betty-Jeanne*!' said Fergus.

'The very same, my boy. The very same. Well, Marcus sailed away to the Emerald Sea, discovered the macadacchio nut and brought it home. I grew a greenhouse full of macadacchio trees from the half dozen nuts he'd returned with, and Crane and Sons' fortune was made.' He shook his head. 'Why we couldn't have left it like that, I'll never know. But then Marcus was never the settling-down type – even when he met your mother, the lovely Lucia.'

Fergus wiped the croissant crumbs away and listened closely.

'She was an orphan, you know,' Uncle Theo said. 'Taught herself to cook. She applied for a job here, which is how the two of them met and fell in love. It was perfect until . . .' Uncle Theo's voice trailed off a second time.

'Until what?' said Fergus, leaning forward.

'The fateful voyage.' Uncle Theo stroked the cover of the log book of the *Betty-Jeanne*. 'But then,' he said, looking back at Fergus, 'you know all about that.'

Chapter Fifteen

'Amazing!' said Fergus, looking up at the enormous trees that towered above them.

'Yes, they truly are,' said Uncle Theo. He patted the nearest macadacchio tree, its orange trunk decorated with big circular knots and whorls. 'The Fateful Voyage Trading Company has five hundred and seven fully grown macadacchio trees here in our greenhouses on Overlook Mountain,' he said proudly.

They had left the gallery of the mountain chalet and taken a cable car across to a nearby mountainside, on which were built three enormous glass-domed greenhouses. Inside each one was a penguin, busy tending to the extraordinary macadacchio trees.

'So you changed the name from *Crane and Sons* to *The Fateful Voyage Trading Company*?' said Fergus, turning to his uncle.

'That's right, my boy. With just me left, I felt *Crane and Sons* didn't quite ring true. And changing the name seemed like a good way to remember your father.'

Fergus paused. 'And my mother?' he asked. 'What happened to her?'

'She never spoke to me again,' said Uncle Theo sadly. 'You see, she blamed me for encouraging your father to set off on that fateful voyage. After he sailed, she never said another word to me – just stayed in her room, weeping. Of course, I had no idea that she'd just found out she was expecting you.' He sighed. 'Then, six months later, the *Betty-Jeanne* shows up and Smollet comes to see me, cool as you like.'

Uncle Theo tutted and shook his head. 'A bad lot, that Smollet, *and* his crew. I blame myself for not checking them out more thoroughly when Marcus first took them on. The trouble was, Fergus, your father was a good man and he always tried to see the good in other people. Smollet took advantage of that.'

'We call him Captain Claw,' said Fergus. 'But only behind his back.'

'A good many others also know him as Captain Claw, as I found out,' said Uncle Theo sharply. 'He's been jailed for piracy and swindling in ports up and down the coast. And apparently he's got six wives.'

'I think I've seen their photographs,' said Fergus. 'My favourite is Mrs Sweetwater Keys.'

'The man's an absolute scoundrel,' said Uncle Theo angrily, 'and his crew are just as bad. Rascals, the lot of them! Lizzie Blood. Red-Beard Spicer. One-Eyed Jack Woodhead. And Short John Gilroy. Nothing but a bunch of pirates! Unfortunately, I found out too late.' He sighed. 'When they returned without Marcus, Smollet – or Captain Claw to you – came to see me. He made me sign over the *Betty-Jeanne* to him, in return for the log.'

'You exchanged the *Betty-Jeanne* for an old book?' said Fergus with surprise.

'But Fergus,' said Theo, 'don't you understand? That old book contains the last thing your father ever wrote. What's a ship compared to that? The blackguard even threatened to burn the log if I didn't agree.

I couldn't let that happen . . .'

Fergus could see tears in his uncle's eyes. Uncle Theo cleared his throat noisily.

'But it was the last straw as far as your mother was concerned,' he went on. 'She packed her bags and vanished in the middle of the night.' He shook his head. 'Dear Lucia,' he said wistfully. 'Does she still end up with a little white moustache after a glass of milk? And sneeze when the sun catches her unawares?'

'Yes,' said Fergus, smiling. 'Yes, she does.' He frowned. 'But Uncle Theo, how did you find her again?' he asked, stepping aside to let Finn, or Bill, or Jackson – he wasn't sure which – waddle past, pushing a wheelbarrow full of macadacchio nuts.

'I didn't,' said Uncle Theo. 'Jackson, here, did. Didn't you, Jackson?'

The penguin nodded and tipped the nuts down a chute set into the greenhouse floor.

'You see, Jackson keeps a scrapbook. Ask him to show it to you some time, it's quite remarkable. Full of cuttings from magazines and newspapers, even books, though I do try to discourage him from tearing pages out of books . . .'

Uncle Theo gave Jackson a stern look. The penguin ignored him, picked up a watering can and waddled off.

'Where was I?'

'The scrapbook,' said Fergus.

'Ah, yes, the scrapbook. Full of things about penguins – pictures, articles, advertisements. If it has a penguin in it, Jackson cuts it out and sticks it in his scrapbook. Well, imagine my surprise when Jackson came to me with a photograph cut out of the *Montmorency Gazette . . .*'

Dr Fassbinder and the cake's creator, Lucia Crane

'The cake!' Fergus exclaimed excitedly. 'The cake with the icing-sugar penguins that Mum baked for Dr Fassbinder's faculty party!'

'The very same,' said Uncle Theo, clapping his hands together. 'I recognized Lucia at once, as did Jackson. It was a simple matter to get in touch with Montmorency Academy and find out that the cake came from Beiderbecker's Bakery. Of course I knew that your mother wanted nothing to do with me, would certainly reject my help if I offered it – and might even disappear again if I wasn't careful. So I sent Jackson to find out more.'

'Jackson?' said Fergus, perplexed. 'Jackson came to Beiderbecker's Bakery?'

'In disguise, obviously,' said Uncle Theo. 'A rather tight-fitting Canada goose suit with mechanical wings. He came  back in a foul temper swearing never again to agree to another of my schemes. Got wedged in a tree in Montmorency Gardens for a day and a half apparently. Still, he saw enough to confirm that Lucia did indeed work behind the bakery counter at Beiderbecker's, and lived in attic rooms next door in

131

Archduke Ferdinand Apartments. He saw something else, too,' Uncle Theo added. 'A boy working behind the cake counter.'

'Me!' said Fergus.

'And the rest, you know,' said Uncle Theo. The legs of his mechanical chair clicked on the shiny paved path as they made their way from the greenhouse back to the cable car. Once inside and descending to the chalet, Uncle Theo continued. 'I had to find out about you, Fergus – and thanks to your co-operation, I did. You can imagine my alarm when I discovered that of the three schools you might have attended, one was the improbably named *School Ship Betty-Jeanne*!

'The thought of you attending such an establishment filled me with horror, Fergus, which was why I had to take such dramatic measures. And from what I've found out about this "school ship" of yours, it looks as if I was right to be so alarmed. Captain Claw is up to no good.'

The cable car came to a smooth halt and the doors slid open. Fergus and Uncle Theo stepped out into the gallery. As they did so, Fergus heard the patter of tiny feet approaching.

'The *Lunchomatic*!'
he exclaimed.

'Just a little ruse of
mine,' said Uncle Theo as

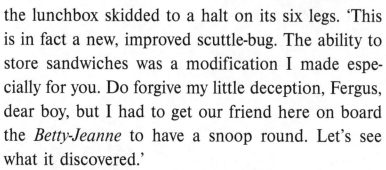

the lunchbox skidded to a halt on its six legs. 'This
is in fact a new, improved scuttle-bug. The ability to
store sandwiches was a modification I made especially for you. Do forgive my little deception, Fergus,
dear boy, but I had to get our friend here on board
the *Betty-Jeanne* to have a snoop round. Let's see
what it discovered.'

Fergus looked down. At their feet was a large sheet
of blank paper spread out on the gallery floor. Uncle
Theo clicked his fingers and the scuttle-bug buzzed
into life, scuttling furiously backwards and forwards
over the paper, ink from its underside making lines
and patterns, seemingly at random.

Slowly, as Fergus watched, the lines began to join
up and a map emerged in front of him – a map, Fergus
realized as the scuttle-bug finished and scuttled over
to stand beside them, of the Emerald Sea and its
islands, all intricately detailed and neatly annotated.

'This,' said Uncle Theo, proudly, 'is an exact copy of the sea chart the scuttle-bug found in Captain Claw's study.' His brows furrowed. 'It was the map your father made on his first voyage to the Emerald Sea – and that black-hearted rogue Claw stole it from him.'

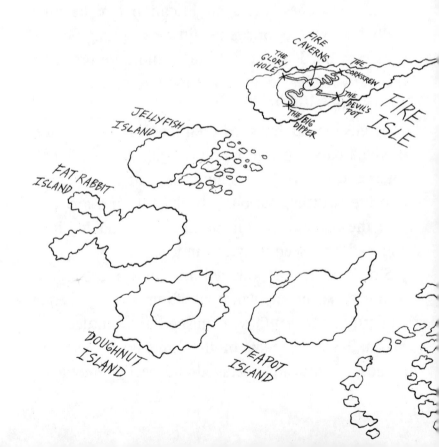

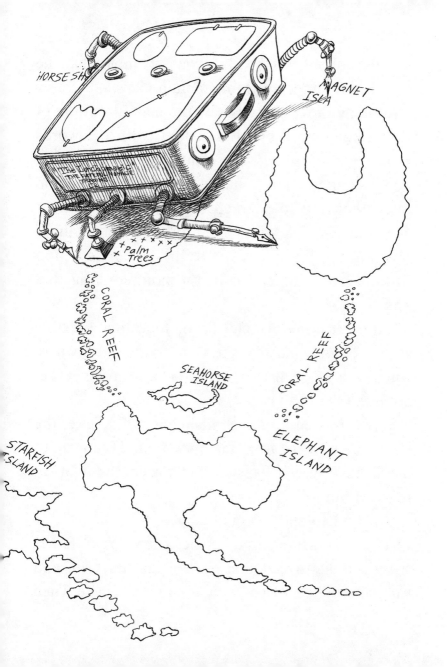

Fergus shook his head. It was no more than he would have expected from Captain Claw.

Looking down, Fergus saw the curved outline of Horseshoe Island by his left foot, with the words *palm trees* and *coral reef* clearly marked. Next to that, Magnet Island, home to the macadacchio trees; then a whole sweep of islands, with names like Starfish, Teapot, Doughnut and Fat Rabbit. They formed the curling tail of the Scorpion Archipelago, and ended in the pointed sting that was Fire Isle.

'Fire Isle,' said Uncle Theo, following Fergus's gaze. 'The only place in the whole wide world where you'll find . . .' Uncle Theo rummaged in his jacket pocket. 'One of these.'

Fergus looked up to see his uncle pull a jewel the size of a gull's egg from his pocket and hold it up to the light, where it dazzled and flashed as if lit up from within.

'A fire diamond!' Fergus gasped.

'The very same,' said Uncle Theo. 'Your father risked his life to get this one on his first trip, and was determined to go back for more.' Uncle Theo pointed to Fire Isle. 'He mapped the location of the fire caverns, as you can see.'

There, at the centre, was the volcano – and down near the bottom the fire caverns were clearly marked. But what really caught Fergus's attention were the four squiggly lines which led from the underground caverns to the outside of the volcano. They each had a name, he saw, his heart leaping into his mouth. *The Glory Hole*, *The Big Dipper*, *The Corkscrew* and *The Devil's Pot*.

Chapter Sixteen

I f anyone, that rainy afternoon in Montmorency Gardens, had been watching from just behind the statue of the Laughing Goat, in the farthest corner amid the brambles and holly bushes, they would have witnessed a most extraordinary sight.

THE LAUGHING GOAT

They would have seen a great silver horse, almost invisible against the grey clouds, gliding down out of the sky on huge, soundless wings. They would have seen the horse land, and a small boy climb from its back, wave it goodbye and hurry off through the gardens - past the clock tower striking five o'clock - in the direction of

138

Boulevard Archduke Ferdinand. And if they had stayed a moment longer, they would have seen the horse flap its great mechanical wings, take off again, and soar away as soundlessly as it had arrived, back towards the distant mountains.

But, on that rainy day in Montmorency Gardens, nobody did see it – for the very simple reason that there was nobody there.

Back at the Archduke Ferdinand Apartment building, Fergus fumbled for his keys and opened the front door. The coast seemed clear. He tiptoed across the marble hall, past the letter boxes and up the stairs to the first floor.

It was all quiet.

He crept round the corner, on up to the second floor, and was just about to continue to the third floor when the door behind him opened. Arturo Squeegie poked his head out.

'Hello, Fergus, old chap,' he said, the toupee on his head sticking up like the back of a snarling dog. 'Haven't seen that dratted cat, have you?'

'No, sorry,' said Fergus, hurrying up the stairs.

'No need to apologize, old man,' Arturo called after him.

Fergus reached the third floor and went on up to the fourth.

Reaching his front door, he put his key in the lock and let himself in. No sooner had he set foot inside than his mother's voice called out from the sitting room.

'Fergus? Fergus, is that you?'

'Yes, Mum,' Fergus replied.

'You didn't wave to me this morning,' she said. 'Did you have a good day at school?'

Fergus came through to the sitting room. His mother was sitting cross-legged on the floor, busy making a long paper-chain of penguins.

'Sorry,' he said. 'I had a lot on my mind. But, yes, I had a very good day.'

'Look what the Fateful Voyage Trading Company sent this time, Fergus.' His mother laughed. 'Penguin paper-chains! And another really big money-order! And the nicest letter. It said I was their most reliable worker ever!'

Fergus smiled.

'Oh, look at you, Fergus,' she said, noticing him properly for the first time. 'You're soaked through! Go and get changed, and I'll make us some hot chocolate. It's new,' she added. 'You'll never guess what it's got in it. Macadacchio nuts!'

Fergus smiled sleepily and went to his room. There, he changed out of his wet clothes and lay on the bed, his uncle's parting words ringing round his head.

'You must go to school tomorrow,' Uncle Theo had told him, 'and warn your friends! Then you must all leave and never go back. Above all, Fergus, dear boy,

don't breathe a word of this to your mother. She mustn't be upset.'

'I won't,' Fergus had promised, climbing onto the flying horse.

'Farewell, Fergus!' Uncle Theo had called. 'It has been lovely meeting you, and remember, I'm always here if you need me.'

When Mrs Crane came in with a mug of hot chocolate, she found her son fast asleep on his quilt. 'Goodnight, Fergus,' she whispered, and kissed his forehead. 'Sweet dreams.'

Chapter Seventeen

eep-peep-peep! Peep-peep-peep! Peep-peep . . .
Fergus awoke to the sound of his alarm clock.
He'd been having the strangest dream.

He'd been on stage with Eugenie Beecham singing
'Daisy's Lament' when Captain Claw, riding an
elephant, had burst into the theatre and chased him
round Montmorency Gardens. He'd only escaped by
disguising himself as Pepe, Antonio the hurdy-gurdy
man's monkey, by wearing Arturo Squeegie's toupee
on his head. Luckily, just as Prince Caspian arrived
and leaped at him, claws glinting, the alarm had gone
off . . .

Peep-peep-peep . . .

Fergus switched it off, climbed out of bed and

hurriedly got dressed. He had to get to school to warn his classmates.

He picked up his backpack, then dropped it again. He wouldn't be needing it – or *Practical Pot-holing for Beginners*. He rushed downstairs and into the kitchen. Propped up against his old lunchbox was a note from his mother.

Can't find new lunchbox. What have you done with it? Use old one today, love Mum.

He wouldn't be needing a lunchbox either, Fergus thought as he dashed down the stairs. He reached the front door just as Miss Jemima Gumm was wheeling her canaries in from their morning constitutional in Montmorency Gardens.

'I saw the funniest thing yesterday afternoon,' she said, in answer to Fergus's cheery 'good morning'. 'I was walking along past Montmorency Gardens when I saw the strangest bird you ever did see, high in the sky and circling the clock tower. Big and silver it was.'

'Probably a seagull, Miss Gumm,' Fergus called back from the front door.

'No, I don't think so,' she said. 'It didn't look like a seagull. More like a . . .' Miss Gumm gave a timid little laugh. 'More like a flying horse.'

Fergus waved to his mother through Beiderbecker's window, then ran full pelt down Boulevard Archduke Ferdinand, across the junction, and on past the theatre and a big billboard crammed with reviews.

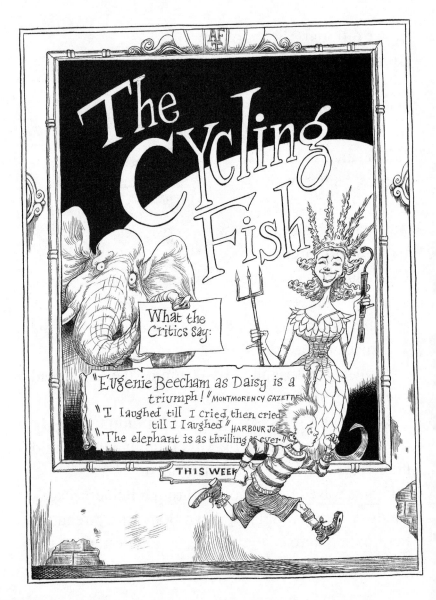

The Cycling Fish, it read. *What the critics say:*

'Eugenie Beecham as Daisy is a triumph!' (*Montmorency Gazette*)

'I laughed till I cried, then cried till I laughed' (*Harbour Journal and Advertiser*)

'The elephant is as thrilling as ever' (*Bayside Observer*)

On through the alleys, Fergus ran, down to the canal side and past Cyclops Point. Perhaps it was the running, perhaps it was the lack of breakfast or the excitement of the last few days – but as he raced towards the quayside, Fergus began to get a distinctly strange, fluttery feeling in the pit of his stomach. It was only when he reached the quay that he realized why.

He gasped. He rubbed his eyes, and looked again. He hadn't imagined it. The *Betty-Jeanne*.

It wasn't there!

In a daze, Fergus ran across the jetty where the school ship should have been. The sign was still in place beside the large iron mooring-ring. *The School Ship Betty-Jeanne* it read, above the picture of the mermaid in a mortar-board. Across it, on a

paper banner pasted to the sign was a notice.

SCHOOL TRIP, it announced. *BACK IN SIX WEEKS*.

'Six weeks!' Fergus exclaimed.

A seagull that had been standing on top of the sign gave a squawk and flew off.

'Oh, no,' groaned Fergus. Bolivia had tried to warn him. 'Don't come to school tomorrow! Don't come to school tomorrow!' she had squawked. She must have known that the pirates were up to no good, but he'd ignored her warnings. And now it was too late! Captain Claw had set sail for Fire Isle – and taken his classmates with him.

Mouse. Horace. Poor, nervous Sylvie. And Spike – brave Spike Thompson. None of them had any idea what awaited them far off in the Emerald Sea.

But he, Fergus Crane, did.

The flutter in his stomach gave way to anger: a boiling, furious anger. Captain Claw and his pirate henchmen were not going to get away with it, not if he could do anything about it.

Turning away, Fergus marched purposefully back in the direction of Boulevard Archduke Ferdinand.

Chapter Eighteen

Fergus sat down on his bed. What *was* he going to do?

He tried to clear his head and concentrate. What would the great explorer and adventurer, Captain Marcus Crane, have done? Or Uncle Theo, for that matter . . ?

Uncle Theo! *He'd* know what to do! He must let Uncle Theo know that the *Betty-Jeanne* had sailed.

But how? Uncle Theo was miles and miles away, high in the mountains . . .

The Fateful Voyage Trading Company! Fergus thought. He could write a note and put it in his mother's latest parcel. What was it this time? Ah, yes, the penguin paper-chains! Uncle Theo would be sure to read it . . .

Fergus dashed downstairs to the sitting room – and groaned. No parcel. His mother must have finished it the previous night and taken it to the Post Office that morning. He sat down on a cushion with a sigh.

Perhaps another parcel had arrived this morning? he suddenly thought. Yes, that's it, another parcel!

Fergus dashed out of the apartment and down the stairs, taking them two at a time. Down in the chilly marble hallway, he skidded to a stop in front of the letter boxes.

His heart sank. There was nothing there either.

He was about to turn away when the front door opened, and in swept Eugenie Beecham in a huge floppy hat and large black glasses. In her arms was a stack of newspapers.

'Fergus! *Daarling!*' she drawled. 'Look! The notices! They lo-oove me! I'm a triumph! It says so, look, here in the *Montmorency Gazette*!' She flapped a paper at Fergus as she swept past.

Fergus gave a half-hearted smile.

'You must come to a performance, Fergus,' Miss Beecham called back. 'You and that delicious mother

of yours. I'll reserve a box just for you,' she said, climbing the stairs.

'What did you say?' said Fergus, his brow furrowing.

'I said you must come to a performance of *The Cycling Fish* with . . .'

'No, after that,' said Fergus.

'I said, I'll reserve a box . . .'

'The box!' shouted Fergus. 'Of course, the box!' It was still in the pocket of his jacket. He would be able to send word to Uncle Theo after all!

Fergus dashed back up the stairs, past an astonished Miss Beecham.

'Fergus? Are you quite all right?' she called up after him.

'I'm fine now, thank you, Miss Beecham,' Fergus called back as he reached his apartment door and rushed inside.

Back in his bedroom, he found his jacket hanging on the hook on the back of his door. With trembling fingers, he reached into the pocket. His hands closed over the little box. He pulled it out gently and looked at it.

The damaged wing hung limply on one side, but the other one looked fine, and the key was still in place. Fergus put the box on his table and turned on his lamp. Examining the wing closely, he noticed that several of the tiny struts beneath its papery surface had been snapped. He turned away and went to the kitchen, returning a moment later with sticky tape and a box of kitchen safety matches.

Carefully taking a match and snapping it to the right length, he fashioned a small splint, which he painstakingly attached to the underside of the wing with the sticky tape. Then, taking the wing tip delicately between thumb and forefinger, he tested it gently, up and down.

It was certainly better than it had been, but there was only one way to find out whether or not it would fly. Fergus pressed the top of the box and the little silver pencil popped up. He tore out the title page of *Practical Pot-holing for Beginners*, took the pencil and began writing beneath the title.

Dear Uncle Theo,

The Betty-Jeanne has sailed. I MUST save my friends. What can I do? PLEASE HELP!

Signed, your long-lost nephew, Fergus.

He folded the paper, popped it inside the little box and clicked the door shut. Then, turning it over, he wound the key until it would turn no more. All Fergus could do now was hope. He crossed to the window, opened it and released the little box, just as the clock in Montmorency Gardens was striking ten o'clock.

The tiny wings of the box beat a little lopsidedly, Fergus had to admit, but the makeshift splint

PRACTICAL
POT-HOLING
FOR BEGINNERS
by
Edward T. Trellis

EDWARD T. TRELLIS

DEAR UNCLE THEO,
THE BETTY-JEANNE HAS SAILED,
I MUST SAVE MY FRIENDS. WHAT
CAN I DO? PLEASE HELP!
SIGNED YOUR LONG-LOST NEPHEW,
Fergus.

seemed to be working. On the brave little box flew, high above the town and on towards the far-off mountains, until Fergus lost sight of it. With a heavy sigh, he flopped down onto his bed, put his arms behind his head and settled down to wait.

Chapter Nineteen

At eight o'clock that evening, Fergus's mother came home. Fergus was in the sitting room.

'Fergus! Fergus! It's the strangest thing!' she said excitedly. 'Sylvie Smith's mother was in the shop this afternoon. She says her Sylvie has gone on a school trip – for six weeks . . .'

'I was going to tell you about that,' Fergus began. 'I missed the boat . . .'

'That's not your fault, dear,' interrupted Mrs Crane. 'From what Mrs Smith was saying, the school gave no one any notice. They just upped and left. Says she's going to have a stern word with that headmaster of yours when they get back!'

'Yes, well,' said Fergus, 'I've been wanting to talk

to you about school as well, Mum . . .'

'You don't have to bother,' said Mrs Crane. 'Not now. It's like I said to Mrs Smith. My Fergus is well out of it. There'll be no more school ships for him.'

'That's true, there won't,' said Fergus.

His mother looked at him curiously.

'I mean,' he said hastily. 'There won't?'

'That's right,' she said. 'It's what I've been trying to tell you, Fergus. The oddest thing . . .'

'Yes?' said Fergus. His mother was starting to worry him now.

'Well, just before Mrs Smith came into Beider-becker's, a parcel arrived outside the shop window. Mr Luscombe from the umbrella shop swears he saw it being delivered by a low-flying Canada goose of all things. If you ask me, the man's a bit cracked in the head. Anyway, there was a parcel there all right, sitting on the pavement and addressed to me. And here it is!'

Mrs Crane flourished a large padded envelope and Fergus's heart leaped as he saw the unmistakable label on its front: *The Fateful Voyage Trading Co.*

'There was a letter inside, along with another money-order,' said Mrs Crane excitedly. 'And Fergus, listen to this . . .' His mother cleared her throat and began.

'Dear Mrs Lucia Crane,

It has been brought to our attention that you have a son of school age. As the son of one of our most valued workers, we would like to offer him the Fateful Voyage Trading Company Scholarship.

As one of our scholarship boys, we would be delighted if he could come and spend some time at the Fateful Voyage Trading Company head-quarters here on Overlook Mountain, both to learn more about the company and to meet us in person.

If the answer is yes, please tick this box □ and travel arrangements will be made.

Yours, with every best wish, Finn, Bill and Jackson, Vice-Presidents, The Fateful Voyage Trading Co.'

'Well, dear?' said Mrs Crane. 'Would you like to go?'

Fergus smiled triumphantly. 'You try and stop me!' he said.

That night the flying box returned, its wing as good as new, with a message.

Dear Fergus, it read. *Am making conventional travel arrangements, as I'm sure you'll understand it wouldn't do to draw too much attention at this stage. Your mother must not be upset.*

Affectionately, your new-found Uncle Theo.

Two days later, an envelope arrived with a train ticket and a timetable and a letter for Mrs Crane.

Thank you for allowing your son to visit Overlook Mountain. Please ensure he has a change of clothes and a waterproof jacket. (Any raincoat with Crane Double Fasteners would be ideal.) We will arrange for him to be met at Snowy Peak Junction.

Best wishes, Finn, Bill and Jackson,

Vice-Presidents, The Fateful Voyage Trading Co.

Mrs Crane waved Fergus goodbye at the station. The dark blue train wound its way round the coast and - with a loud whistle - rattled into the long, dark tunnel through the mountains.

On the other side at last, Fergus found himself crossing farmland, with fields and meadows and orchards, and bridges over fast-running rivers, and on through dark forests and sprawling cities towards the distant mountains where his Uncle Theo lived. The journey seemed so much longer by train than by flying horse, Fergus thought; but he had plenty of sandwiches and a Thermos of hot chocolate in his backpack – and besides, there was so much to think about . . .

Finally, early the next morning, Fergus woke up to find the little train chugging into Snowy Peak Junction. He stretched, rubbed his eyes, looked out of the window – and there waiting for him on the platform were Uncle Theo and the penguins.

'Fergus, my dear boy!' Uncle Theo exclaimed as Fergus climbed down from the train. 'Breakfast is ready and waiting for us in the gallery. Come, we have important plans to make!'

Chapter Twenty

Far below him, as the flying horse soared on, the patchwork landscape abruptly gave way to water and Fergus found himself flying over an endless expanse of slate-grey ocean. Cold, misty air swirled round him. Sometimes the cloud thickened and the horse would fly up above it, its silvery hoofs seeming to gallop over the fluffy white drifts; sometimes the sky cleared, and Fergus had to cling on tightly round the flying horse's neck as it swooped back down towards the sea. He saw their own shadow flitting across the rolling surface as they passed overhead.

Soon there was nothing but water all round him. Whichever way he looked – left, right, behind and

ahead – the mighty ocean continued unbroken to the horizon. There were no ships to be seen; no fishing boats, no sailing ships, no yachts . . .

Fergus trembled. He had never been so far out to sea before. He was completely and utterly alone. If anything should happen to the flying horse, then he and it would be lost forever, swallowed up without a trace by the endless ocean . . .

It had felt so different that bright sunny morning when Uncle Theo had waved him off from the mountain chalet. The old inventor had spent the previous two weeks working on the flying horse, poring over the charts the scuttle-bug had provided, and adjusting the mechanism in the creature's great metal head.

Fergus had spent most of the time with Finn, Bill and Jackson in the green-houses, learning all about the art of growing macadacchio nuts. And it was a fine art, as Fergus quickly discovered. The roots of the trees had to be carefully watered, the leaves dusted daily, and the temperature in the greenhouses monitored at all times.

At the end of the two weeks, Fergus was quite an expert, even helping Finn with the wind-up gramophone he used to play soothing music to the giant trees. Their favourite record, or so Finn maintained, was 'Daisy's Lament' from *The Cycling Fish*, sung by Dame Ottaline Ffarde.

In addition, Fergus practised flying the winged horse. Every evening, after the day's work in the greenhouses had been finished, but before the sun had set, Fergus would climb up into the saddle and the great metal creature would soar up into the sky.

'You're a natural, my boy,' Uncle Theo had laughed at the end of the first week, as Fergus and the horse came gently back to earth.

'That's not what you said last week,' said Fergus, jumping from the saddle, 'and I haven't fallen off once!'

'I had the horse set on *automatic rider* for your own safety, Fergus, but that was before I realized what a quick learner you are,' said Uncle Theo. 'I think we can lose this, now.' He removed the *DO NOT TOUCH* sign from the reins. 'It's all yours, my boy!'

For the following week, Fergus had the time of his life as he mastered swooping dips, wheeling turns and hair-raising loop-the-loops, all at a flick of the reins.

Finally, the day of departure had arrived.

'Fergus,' Uncle Theo had said sternly. 'I've done all I can. The horse will take you to Fire Isle, so you don't need to use the reins. Once you're there, of course, you may ride where you will. But you must promise me this, Fergus. You are to engage in no dangerous heroics. Think of your poor dear mother waiting for you at home.'

Fergus had nodded solemnly.

'If the *Betty-Jeanne* has made it to Fire Isle,' his uncle had continued, 'then you must go straight to Captain Claw and offer him the scuttle-bug in return for the safety of your classmates. He might be a black-hearted pirate, but he's no fool. He'll realize that the scuttle-bug will do the job every bit as well as your poor comrades ever could, Tunnel Exercise or no Tunnel Exercise.'

Fergus had nodded again.

'Remember, Fergus,' Uncle Theo had called after him as the flying horse rose into the air. 'No heroics!'

As the great winged beast flapped on across the ocean his Uncle Theo's words came back to him, and Fergus shook his head. The last thing he felt right now, out here all alone, was heroic.

Fergus never discovered just how long he travelled, for somewhere over the seemingly endless expanse, the first day blurred into the next, with a long cold night in between. When he was tired, he slept, clinging on tightly round the flying horse's neck; when he was hungry or thirsty, he sampled the exotic rations and delicious hot chocolate dispensed by the scuttle-bug. Finally – after what Fergus would later describe as 'the longest flight of my life' – he spotted land.

As they drew closer, Fergus saw that there were in fact two rocky islands coming to meet one another, divided by a channel of water. They must be approaching the Stormy Straits, the gateway to the Emerald Sea.

The flying horse flew into the oncoming wind, its wings beating powerfully, and it wasn't long before Fergus was able to see a patch of almost luminous green far in the distance. Closer and closer it came until, all at once, the air grew still and below him the sea glinted like a vast slab of polished jade.

And there were the islands, Fergus saw, his heart leaping: Horseshoe Island, just as he'd imagined it; and Magnet Island, its entire surface covered in dark green trees; and a small rocky island which looked like a tiny seahorse. Further they flew, the air warm and scented with spices and herbs. The sun had passed its highest point and was coming down in the sky far ahead.

The archipelago came into view, looking even more like a scorpion from above than it did on the map. Fergus counted off the islands, his heart thumping with excitement, as the great winged horse followed the scorpion's long clawed legs, the curve of its back and on, along its tail. Fergus's heart missed a beat.

'There it is,' Fergus whispered as the last island of all came into view. There was no doubt. It was Fire Isle.

Curved, pointed, fringed with glittering sand and with a tall, cone-shaped volcano glowing at its centre, the island seemed to sparkle like a jewel in the half-light of the setting sun. The flying horse began to descend in the sky.

As it came lower, Fergus pulled sharply on the reins. There was a familiar *click* from inside the horse's head as he took control. He tugged to the left, and they circled the island – once, twice – with Fergus peering down through the trees and scouring the beaches, with their white sand and orange and grey speckled boulders, for any sign of footprints. Lower still they came, until he could see the coconuts in the palms and the bulbous red and black nuts hanging from the spreading branches of the macadacchio trees that grew there.

Interesting, he thought; but not what he was looking for. He steered the horse back to the shore-line and yanked hard down on the reins. Abruptly, the flying horse flew back up into the sky. It soared over the rocky outcrop before it, and the island beyond opened up.

Fergus gasped with surprise.

On the other side of the rocks was a small, natural harbour. And there, tied up to a pinnacle of rock was a ship. Fergus stared down at the tall masts and the furled sails.

It was the *Betty-Jeanne*.

Chapter Twenty-one

The flying horse swooped down and landed on the foredeck almost without a sound. Fergus gratefully dismounted, stretched and looked round. The ship seemed deserted.

'Hello!' he called. 'Hello, is there anybody aboard? It's me, Fergus!'

From above his head, high up in the parrot's nest, there came a familiar squawk.

'Fergus! Fergus!' Bolivia's voice floated down. 'You've come back! You've come back!'

The parrot emerged from her hiding place and swooped down to join Fergus on deck.

'They've gone! They've gone!' Bolivia squawked, settling on Fergus's arm. 'To the big mountain!

Boom! Boom!'

'Never mind that,' said Fergus, a look of concern on his face. 'What's happened to you, Bolivia?' The parrot looked decidedly bedraggled – her wing feathers ruffled, bare patches at her neck, and with several tail feathers missing entirely.

'Captain Claw! Captain Claw!' said Bolivia. 'Eat me! Cook me! Parrot stew!'

'The big bully!' said Fergus hotly. 'He doesn't deserve a fine bird like you.' He smoothed down Bolivia's feathers. 'Here, I've got a real treat for you,' he said, and clicked his fingers.

The scuttle-bug jumped down from the saddle and stood beside him.

'What would you say to a bowl of hot chocolate with macadacchio nuts?'

*

A cold wind was blowing round the top of the volcano. It hit the hot, smoky air emerging from the volcanic crater, mingled, and caused dark, gold-edged clouds to gather in the sky far above.

On the lip of the mighty volcano stood Captain Claw, a whistle in his hand and a metal bucket on the end of an iron chain hanging from his claw-like hook. Further down, where the jungle lapped at the volcano's steep slopes, were four pairs of individuals – each made up of a pirate and a child – standing beside four tiny pot-holes.

'When I blow the whistle!' Captain Claw roared. 'The Tunnel Exercise will begin!'

He glared down at his crew. Lizzie Blood stood with a length of rope attached to a harness worn by a shocked-looking Sylvie Smith. Horace Tucker tried to smile, his rope held by a yawning Red-Beard Spicer; while Short John Gilroy scowled and yanked at Spike Thompson's harness, causing the boy to scowl back. Mouse looked down at her feet. Beside her One-Eyed Jack Woodhead smiled nastily.

'When you've filled this bucket with fire diamonds,' Captain Claw bellowed, the long length of chain jangling against the metal bucket as he held it up, 'you are to tug twice on the rope. Your teachers will then pull you to the surface. Is everybody ready?'

The pirates all nodded and pushed their children towards the pot-holes. Captain Claw smiled malevolently and winked at One-Eyed Jack, who laughed. Then he turned back to the volcano's edge, placed the whistle in his mouth, and blew.

When Fergus heard Captain Claw's bellowed commands echoing far above his head, he groaned miserably. Uncle Theo had told him to offer the scuttle-bug in exchange for the safe release of his friends, but once again he had arrived too late. Horace and Mouse, Sylvie and Spike had already been despatched down the tunnels to carry out Captain Claw's dirty work for him.

Fergus crawled forward, the little machine buzzing and clicking softly in his backpack. He had to know exactly what was going on. Before he'd gone far, he heard a noise to his left. There was someone there.

Taking care to remain silent himself, Fergus crept towards the noise. He paused, parted the branches and peered out. Red-Beard Spicer was just ahead of him, standing beside a pothole. Fergus frowned. The pirate was feeding a length of rope down into the pot-hole, letting the rope slip through his fingers.

Fergus stared at the rope in horror. At the end of it was one of his friends – Horace, if he had got his bearings right and this was indeed *The Glory Hole*.

Just then, the pot-hole gurgled and belched, and a cloud of pungent yellow smoke billowed up into the air. Fergus gagged. It was *The Glory Hole*, all right!

Poor Horace, he thought. He'll have to be better than ever at holding his breath down there if . . .

Fergus's jaw dropped as he saw the frayed end of the rope suddenly flick through Spicer's hands. The man made no effort to stop it. Instead, a bored smile playing on his lips, he put his hands nonchalantly in his pockets.

'*Glory Hole* away!' he called up to Captain Claw.

His voice was joined by the shouts of the other pirates.

'*Big Dipper* away!'

'*Corkscrew* away!'

'*Devil's Pot* away!'

Fergus's blood was boiling. Captain Claw and the pirates had no intention of pulling the children to safety after the iron bucket was full. The ropes were just for show; a cruel joke . . .

No heroics! Uncle Theo's voice came back to him once more. *No heroics!*

With a sigh, Fergus turned and disappeared into the jungle, back the way he'd come.

Chapter Twenty-two

The pirates were clustered round Captain Claw at the lip of the volcano, watching intently as he lowered the metal bucket into the crater's smoking depths. The iron chain clinked and clanked against his clawlike hook. Far below, the children were crawling towards the fire caverns, unaware that the pirates had abandoned them to their fate.

'Scurvy deck-swabbers!' spat Lizzie Blood. 'I'm glad to be rid of them!'

'Me, too, Lizzie, me old love,' said Red-Beard Spicer in a bored voice. 'Pot-holing for beginners? Pot-holing for *losers*, more like!'

One-Eyed Jack Woodhead folded his tattooed arms and gave a nasal laugh. 'No more Tunnel Exercise, that's for sure!'

'And we'll be rich,' sniggered Short John Gilroy, wiping his hands excitedly on his filthy apron. 'Rich beyond our wildest dreams!'

'Come on, come on,' growled Captain Claw impatiently. 'What's taking the little beggars so blasted long?'

Just then, the chain gave a slight jolt. Then another one. And another, and another . . .

'The little beauties!' chuckled Captain Claw. 'That's the job. Fill the bucket with those fire diamonds right up to the top, then we can be on our way.'

He laughed again, and the others all joined him in a rising chorus of hideous cackles – which, the next moment, collapsed into wheezy splutters and choking coughs as the volcano began belching out thick clouds of sulphurous smoke. A while later, the chain in Captain Claw's one good hand and less good metal claw gave a sharp lurch, followed by another.

'It's full!' cried Captain Claw. 'Quick, everyone! Help me haul it up!'

The pirates jumped to it, forming a line and grabbing the chain like the seasoned seafarers they were, as if raising a sail. Captain Claw moved to the back and gripped the end of the chain.

'One, two, three and *heave*!' he roared. *'Heave! Heave! Heave . . .'*

Slowly, the heavy iron bucket rose through the clouds of eye-watering, breath-snatching fumes.

'Heave!' roared Captain Claw for the final time as the bucket, glowing faintly from the intense heat, swung into view.

At that same moment, from high above him, there came the sound of beating wings and the clouds of smoke parted briefly to reveal a mighty winged horse hovering directly overhead. Captain Claw and the pirates stared at it, open-mouthed.

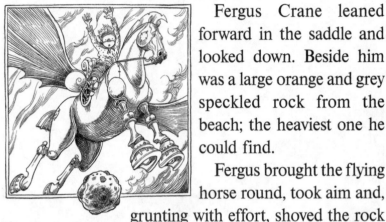 Fergus Crane leaned forward in the saddle and looked down. Beside him was a large orange and grey speckled rock from the beach; the heaviest one he could find.

Fergus brought the flying horse round, took aim and, grunting with effort, shoved the rock off the saddle. With a whistle – oddly small and soft for something so big and hard – it hurtled down through the air. Fergus watched it, his heart in his mouth, his breath held, his fingers crossed for good luck . . .

Clang!

It landed loudly and heavily on the top of the bucketful of fire diamonds and the air echoed with the sound of chains rattling through grasping hands as the bucket plunged back down into the depths of the volcano.

'NO!' roared Captain Claw, unwilling to let his precious fire diamonds disappear.

He gripped the chain and held on with all his might. In front of him, the other pirates did the same, digging their heels – and one wooden stump – into the crumbly ash at the top of the volcano.

But it was no good. The bucket was too heavy for them. One by one, they were tugged forwards to the lip of the volcanic crater, howling and cursing and uttering the foulest of oaths – but refusing to let go.

'Hell's haddocks!' howled Red-Beard Spicer, disappearing over the edge.

'By Satan's starfish!' cursed One-Eyed Jack Woodhead, following him.

'*Heave*, blast you!' Captain Claw screeched, his head back, his mouth grimacing, and every muscle in his body straining.

'Blood and gunpowder!' screeched Lizzie Blood as she, too, abruptly disappeared into the crater.

'Pilchard stew!' cried Short John Gilroy, joining her a moment after.

'I . . . won't . . . let . . . go . . .' Captain Claw snarled through clenched teeth. 'The fire diamonds are mine . . . *Aaaargh!*' he screamed as he followed the bucket and the other pirates over the edge and down, down into the fiery heart of the mighty volcano.

Chapter Twenty-three

The flying horse landed on the slope of the volcano beside the nearest pot-hole. Fergus jumped down and rushed to the entrance.

'Hello?' he called.

'*Hello . . . hello . . . hello . . .*' his own voice echoed back.

'Is there anyone there? Horace? Mouse? Sylvie? Spike? Can you hear me?'

'*. . . hear me? . . . hear me?*'

It was no good. Uncle Theo might have told him not to take part in any heroics, but his friends were in danger. He couldn't just leave them there, could he? Without a second thought, Fergus fell to his knees and crawled into the hole.

The first thing that struck him was the air. It was oven-hot and so thick with smoke that Fergus could barely see his hands in front of his face. Ahead of him, the tunnel seemed to plunge down almost vertically into blackness.

Slowly and carefully, he lowered himself down, his feet and shoulders braced against the jagged rock. Soon he found himself in complete darkness, the sound of his breathing loud in his head against the distant roaring of the volcano far below.

The deeper Fergus went, the hotter it became, and the pungent fumes caught in his throat and made his eyes water. It took all his strength and concentration to stop

himself from slipping and plunging down into the inky depths.

Not even Tunnel Exercise had prepared him for this.

Suddenly, the rock beneath his left foot crumbled and fell away in a clattering shower of rock shards. Fergus felt himself falling.

'UNNKH!'

The wind was completely knocked out of him as he hit the rocky floor at the bottom of the shaft.

Shaking his head to clear his thoughts, Fergus looked about him. Ahead, the narrow tunnel snaked away, its walls bathed in the fiery glow of the volcano.

The vertical drop; the levelling out into a narrow tunnel . . . Fergus knew this place. It was bigger, hotter and far more frightening than the tunnel in the ballast, but there was no doubt. This was *The Devil's Pot*.

'Spike! Spike!' Fergus called. 'Spike, are you there?'

There was no reply, only the constant roaring noise of the fiery volcano.

Taking a deep breath and summoning up all his courage, Fergus crawled forward, towards the sound of the inferno. The tunnel grew narrower and narrower. Fergus hurt his elbows and shins as he scrambled and squeezed his way along it. But though twice as hot and four times as long as the tunnel in the ballast, he was determined that the real *Devil's Pot* was not going to defeat him.

At last, grazed and gasping for breath, Fergus squeezed round the last bend and stopped. In front of him was the most spectacular sight he had ever seen.

He was standing in a huge vaulted chamber that shimmered with dazzling light. Reds, purples, iridescent blues, luminous yellows and greens all danced and swirled in a hypnotic kaleidoscope of colour. The walls and ceiling seemed to be made up of countless intricate crystals, as if the entire cave had been dipped in sugar.

Fergus reached out and touched the cavern wall. With a faint click, a crystal fell into his hand, and Fergus found himself staring at a flawless, perfectly-formed fire diamond.

'Fergus?' came a voice behind him. 'Fergus, is that you?'

Fergus spun round and squinted into the dazzling brightness. Someone was stumbling towards him along the ledge that ran round the cavern walls; someone small, someone with a black bob and dark eyes . . .

'Mouse!' he cried.

'It *is* you!' said Mouse. 'Oh, Fergus, they cut the rope! I could have died!'

Fergus hugged his friend and turned to see Spike and Horace hurrying towards them from opposite sides of the cavern.

'Fergus, what are *you* doing here?' said Horace, his face and clothes black with soot.

'It's a long story, Fergus said. 'I'll tell you later. He paused. 'Where's Sylvie?' he said.

'She was with me a moment ago,' said Spike, looking round. 'She's in a bit of a state. *The Corkscrew* really took it out of her.'

'*She's* in a state!' said Fergus. 'What about you, Spike?'

There was a nasty gash on Spike's forehead, his knees were grazed and bloody, and he was clutching his right arm tightly to his chest.

'Oh, it's nothing,' he said bravely. 'Just a little fall

back there in *The Devil's Pot.*'

Just then, there came a piercing scream. 'Help!
Help!'

'Sylvie?' Spike shouted. 'Sylvie, where *are* you?'

'Here,' she called back. 'Hurry! Please!'

'It came from over there,' said Fergus, peering
through the bright, shimmering light. 'Quick, follow
me!'

They made their way as quickly as they could
along the narrow ledge, fire diamonds clinking and
dropping to the ground as they brushed past. All at
once, Fergus came to an abrupt halt.

He could go no further. The ledge in front of him
had fallen away. Far below, a great lake of molten
lava seethed, belching out clouds of acrid smoke.

'Fergus? Fergus, is that you?' came Sylvie's tearful
voice. 'I'm stuck. I'm stuck, Fergus.'

On either side of her, the ledge had given way and
Sylvie was marooned on the one narrow section that
remained. Below her, the molten lava bubbled and
plopped; beside her, a crack was slowly zigzagging
across the centre of the jutting ledge, threatening to
break it off at any moment and send the whole lot

hurtling down into the infernal cauldron.

'Stand back,' said Fergus in a whisper to Horace, Mouse and Spike. 'I'll try to calm her down.'

Spike for one looked as if he wanted to launch himself across the gap to rescue Sylvie there and then, despite his injured arm. But Mouse put a hand on his shoulder.

'Don't do anything silly, Spike, that ledge could give way at any moment,' she said. 'Let Fergus handle this.'

Spike turned away and kicked the cavern wall with frustration. A shower of glittering fire diamonds cascaded down into the lava below.

'I . . . I can't move,' Sylvie wailed, tears streaming down her face. 'My legs won't work.'

'Listen to me, Sylvie,' Fergus called, trying to sound calm and reassuring. 'You have to jump across to us. Horace and I will catch you. You must be very brave, Sylvie, and trust us.'

'I can't,' wailed Sylvie, the tears coming thick and fast. 'Oh, I'm so stupid and useless . . .'

'You *can*, Sylvie,' Fergus insisted. 'You're not stupid, you're not useless. You're the best in gym class, everyone knows that. Why, you can jump further than any of us. You know you can . . .'

'You can certainly jump further than me, you long-legged giraffe!' urged Horace, trying to smile. 'But I'm better at catching any day. Come on, Sylvie.' He spread his arms wide. 'You can do it!'

'Close your eyes and imagine you're back in gym class,' said Fergus.

The crack on Sylvie's ledge

inched towards her. Sylvie closed her eyes.

'Then take a deep breath.'

Sylvie took a deep breath.

'Now . . . *Jump*!'

Sylvie let out a little squeal and jumped. The next moment, the ledge gave way and hurtled down into the molten lake of lava below.

'*Gotcha!*' cried Horace and Fergus together as Sylvie landed in a heap on top of them. For a moment they remained frozen in a big hug, Mouse and Spike included.

'I knew you could do it!' came Fergus's voice from the midst of the huddle.

'You saved me again, Fergus,' Sylvie replied.

'I'm the Spare,' said Fergus. 'That's my job!'

Just then, there came an ominous creak, and the ledge beneath their feet gave a sickening lurch. Behind them, in the direction from which they'd come, another section of ledge collapsed in a glittering shower of fire diamonds. The molten lava boiled and spat with renewed fury, and the little group was enveloped in great billowing clouds of sulphurous smoke.

'That's torn it!' exclaimed Spike.

'We're trapped!' gasped Mouse.

'What are we going to do?' Horace croaked.

'Fergus?' wailed Sylvie.

'I . . . I . . .' stuttered Fergus. 'I . . . don't . . . know.'

Whenever Fergus thought back to that awful moment – the sulphurous smoke, the bubbling lava, the blinding light and suffocating heat – he could never quite remember *exactly* what happened next. And when they talked of it later, none of the children could agree.

'One moment you were there, Mouse,' Sylvie remembered. 'The next, you'd gone.'

'No, *I* was there and *you* disappeared,' Mouse interrupted.

'I thought it was you taking my hand and leading me towards the tunnel,' said Horace.

'I thought it was *you*,' Spike replied.

'I remember being lifted up,' said Fergus. 'And the next thing, I was climbing up a tunnel – and I remember thinking, *this* isn't *The Devil's Pot.*'

'Or *The Corkscrew*,' said Sylvie.

'Or *The Glory Hole*,' laughed Horace.

'And certainly not *The Big Dipper*,' added Mouse.

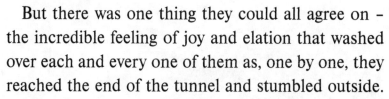

But there was one thing they could all agree on – the incredible feeling of joy and elation that washed over each and every one of them as, one by one, they reached the end of the tunnel and stumbled outside.

Night had fallen, and a huge full moon shone down brightly on the clearing where they had emerged. Fergus collapsed to the ground and gulped in huge lungfuls of air. Beside him, the others did the same. Spike was the first to climb to his feet.

'We did it!' he exclaimed. 'We escaped!' And the five boys and girls cheered so loudly that the parakeets roosting in the nearby trees flapped their wings and screeched indignantly.

It was only when they stopped cheering and sat down once more, that Fergus realized they were not alone. Looking up, he found himself staring into the amused eyes of a weather-beaten figure, his wild hair, huge beard and ragged clothes silhouetted against the moon, making him look like a neglected scarecrow.

'Lucky for you that I found you when I did,' the man said.

Fergus stood up unsteadily. 'Who are you?' he asked gently.

'Yes,' said the others, gathering round. 'Who *are* you?'

'A poor shipwrecked sailor,' the man replied. 'I must have been shipwrecked many years ago, but I'm afraid I've no memory of that at all. I woke up on the beach back there after a terrible eruption, and I've been here ever since. Know every inch of Old Smoky up there, including the fire caverns, and if there's one thing I've learned, it's that fire caverns are no place for children. Can't imagine what you thought you were doing in there.'

'Fire diamonds,' said Fergus. 'They're the cause of all this. And I wish I'd never heard of them!'

The other children all nodded their agreement, and Sylvie blew her nose loudly.

'Fire diamonds?' said the man. 'You mean these?' He emptied his ragged pockets and held out his hands. They gleamed with fiery, glowing stones. 'Oh, they're pretty enough,' he said, 'but absolutely useless. You can't eat them for a start.' He grinned.

'Now the macadacchio nut, that's a different story. Worth its weight in gold, it is. Absolutely delicious. And the strangest thing is, every time I taste one I get the most peculiar feeling – though I can't quite put my finger on it . . .'

'You'd better come with us,' said Fergus, taking the man's hand gently.

'Why?' said the man.

'Because,' said Fergus, 'you're a shipwrecked sailor, and we've got a ship to sail.'

The stranger smiled. 'Then I'm your man!' he laughed.

Chapter Twenty-four

B ack aboard the *Betty-Jeanne*, the stranger soon made himself at home. Taking his place at the wheel, he bellowed out for the sails to be unfurled and the anchor to be raised. And as the ship leaped forward, he brought it round until the volcanic island was behind them and the sparkling, moonlit Emerald Sea in front.

'Full sail ahead!' he cried. 'And steady as she goes!'

At the stern of the ship, Fergus raised a telescope to his eye and looked back at Fire Isle. The top of the volcano glowed in the darkness like a huge lamp, gently illuminating everything about it; the tall mountain, the dense forest and the strip of sandy beach, with its orange and grey speckled boulders.

He felt a twinge as he thought of the pirates. If only their greed hadn't stopped them from letting go of the bucket . . . Then again, he remembered, they'd been only too willing to sacrifice all his classmates for the fire diamonds. Fergus snapped the telescope shut. Bolivia fluttered down and landed on his shoulder.

'Hot chocolate! Hot chocolate!' she squawked.

The scuttle-bug buzzed and clicked as it scuttled up to join them. Fergus had had the presence of mind to send it into the volcano before they left, and now, as well as the last of the hot chocolate, the bug was crammed full of fire diamonds.

He joined the stranger up at the helm, and watched the waves parting as the *Betty-Jeanne* ploughed through them. Bolivia was still perched on his shoulder, her head tucked under her wing; the winged horse was down below deck, safely stowed in the gym – while the other girls and boys had each snuggled down in one of the pirates' hammocks, and were fast asleep.

'It's funny,' said the stranger. 'It's almost as though I know this ship.'

Fergus smiled. 'I was just thinking that,' he said.

A week later, the wind rose and the sea grew choppier as they approached the Stormy Straits, but the *Betty-Jeanne* was equal to the changing conditions. With its sails full, it hurtled down the straits and out into the great ocean beyond.

The rest of the voyage was uneventful. Horace fell overboard a few times, and they all took it in turns to ride the winged horse. The stranger – whom they all just called 'Captain' – shaved off his beard, got Mouse to cut his hair, and ended up looking quite presentable. At least, Fergus thought so. But then he was biased.

A fortnight later, they spotted the tall buildings of the city.

'There it is!' shouted Horace excitedly. 'We're back!'

'Home!' cried Sylvie, and burst into tears.

The *Betty-Jeanne* entered the harbour and, with pinpoint accuracy, the captain brought her round into the empty mooring bay. Horace jumped across to the jetty and tied the rope tightly round the steel bollard. The gangplank was lowered, and the others streamed ashore. Horace tore the notice from the school sign.

'"School trip" indeed!' he said. 'Wait till my dad hears about this! Mind you, it's true,' he added, 'we have been away for six weeks exactly.'

'*There* you are, Sylvie!' came a loud voice. 'Did you have a nice time, love? Ooh, you do look well! Doesn't she look well, Cyril?'

Mr and Mrs Smith bustled up to the quayside, followed closely by Mrs Maas, Mr and Mrs Tucker, laughing loudly and clapping Horace on the back, and old man Thompson, who gave Spike a gruff hug.

'Don't forget,' called Fergus, waving. 'See you all tomorrow, bright and early.'

'What about me?' said the captain.

'Secure the ship,' said Fergus. 'Then you're coming home with me. Both of you!' he added, as Bolivia landed on his shoulder.

Chapter Twenty-Five

A t the tall, pointing statue of General Montmorency, Fergus and the captain turned left and headed up into the labyrinth of narrow alleys. They hurried through square after familiar square, past fountains and sculptures, flower-stalls and candy-booths, and small, candle-lit shops selling intricately carved wooden figures.

Turning right at old Mother Bleeny's bagel-stand, Fergus and the captain emerged onto the

GENERAL MONTMORENCY

212

bustling Boulevard Archduke Ferdinand with its tall, slightly shabby buildings. Wall-eyed Ned was in his usual spot in front of the Archduke Ferdinand Theatre. Head down, he was marching back and forth, the sandwich-board strapped to his body advertising the new show in town. This month it was a family melodrama entitled *Lady Lilian's Dilemma*.

'Afternoon, Ned,' Fergus called.

'Afternoo . . . *Fergus!* You're back!' cried Ned, seizing his hand and pumping it up and down.

Further along the road, the air swirled with mournful music, which suddenly stopped as old Antonio rushed up, Pepe on his shoulder, and embraced Fergus.

'Welcome back, Fergus!' he cried.

 They continued past familiar shops. *Madame Aimee's Wedding Gowns. H.H. Luscombe's Umbrellas. Le Café Rondel. Joshua Berwick: Bespoke Tailor. Karpff*, the jeweller's.

Outside every one, Fergus's hand was shaken, his back slapped, and his hair ruffled; sometimes all three at once.

'It must be nice to be missed like this,' said the captain thoughtfully. 'And to know there's a place where you're known and loved.'

'Come on,' said Fergus. 'We're nearly there.'

They arrived at Beiderbecker's Bakery. Fergus pressed his nose against the window and peered through the displays of walnut eclairs and almond meringues at the counter. His mother turned from serving an old woman with a fat dachshund and, seeing him, gave a little cry of joy.

Beiderbecker's Bakery

Fergus waved. His mother waved back, then gave a scream - high and piercing. She had spotted the captain.

Fergus turned to his father. 'You wanted to know what it's like to be missed, and to know a place where you're known and loved, didn't you?'

The captain nodded, a strange expression on his face.

'Well, come inside,' said Fergus, 'and you'll find out!'

From the *Montmorency Gazette*, 21 August:

CULINARY WONDER TAKES OVER BEIDERBECKER'S BAKERY

Today the Beiderbecker Bakery was purchased by Mrs Lucia Crane, wife of the fire diamond millionaire, Captain Marcus Crane.

Mrs Lucia Crane, famous in her own right as the inventor of *Archduke Ferdinand's Classic Florentines*, said that taking over the renamed 'Fateful Voyage Bakery' was 'the second happiest day of my life!'

From an interview in *Starlight* with Miss Eugenie Beecham:

'Of course, my portrayal of Daisy in *The Cycling Fish* is still talked about in theatrical circles. I work less now, however, as I'm very involved in my Tenants' Association, the Fateful Voyage Apartment Building. It's owned by the Crane family – wonderful people – and is by far the most fashionable address in town!'

From The Fateful Voyage Trading Co.:

Dear Wall-eyed Ned and Antonio (the hurdy-gurdy man),

We are pleased to award you 'The Fateful Voyage Trading Co. Grant for Theatrical Achievements in an Open Air Setting', and wish you both a comfortable and prosperous retirement,

With very best wishes,

Finn Bill Jackson

and

X

Finn, Bill, Jackson and Bolivia,
Vice-Presidents, The Fateful Voyage Trading Co.

From *The Scowling Mermaid*, school magazine of the
school ship *Betty-Jeanne*:

We are pleased to welcome the new
headmaster, Dr Fassbinder, aboard, and
a new music teacher, Madame Lavinia.
Headboy, Fergus Crane, said, "Dr
Fassbinder is what I call a real teacher".

Horace Tucker is looking for volunteers
for the school production of *The Cycling
Fish*.

From the Archduke Ferdinand Museum catalogue:

'THE QUESTING MUSE'

An exhibition of portraits by the late Rachel Dubois,

from the collection of Theodore and Marcus Crane.

In the new 'Fateful Voyage' wing of the museum.

'SELF PORTRAIT IN A RAINCOAT'

From the *Harbour High Society* magazine (torn out and put in Jackson's scrapbook):

Seagull ABOUT TOWN

FIRE DIAMOND FIVE ADD SPARKLE TO SHOW

The famous 'Fire Diamond Five' attended a glitzy opening of the Rachel Dubois exhibition at the Archduke Ferdinand Museum last night. The young millionaires, from left to right: Sylvie Smith, 'Mouse' Maas, Horace Tucker, Fergus Crane, 'Spike' Thompson, and an unidentified friend.

And from a flying box which arrived at midnight last night:

Dear Fergus

Please come quickly, the penguins are in grave DANGER!

your loving uncle,

Theo

PAUL STEWART

PAUL STEWART is a highly regarded author of books
for young readers – everything from picture books to
football stories, fantasy and horror. Several of his
books are published by Random House Children's
Books, including *The Wakening,* which was selected as
a Pick of the Year by the Federation of Children's
Book Groups. Together with Chris Riddell, he is
co-creator of the bestselling Edge Chronicles series,
which is now available in over twenty languages.

CHRIS RIDDELL is an accomplished graphic artist who has illustrated many acclaimed books for children, including *Pirate Diary* by Richard Platt, for which he won the 2001 Kate Greenaway Medal, *Something Else* by Kathryn Cave, which was shortlisted for the Kate Greenaway Medal and the Smarties Prize and won the Unesco Award, and *Castle Diary* by Richard Platt, which was Highly Commended both for the 1999 Kate Greenaway Medal and for the V&A Illustrations Award. Together with Paul Stewart, he is co-creator of the bestselling Edge Chronicles series, which is now available in over twenty languages.

EDWARD T. TRELLIS

EDWARD T. TRELLIS is a widely acclaimed pot-holer
and dramatist who has explored many caves, canyons
and crevices, as well as writing some of the most
popular musical farces of recent years. These include
Lady Lilian's Dilemma, shortlisted for the Harbour
Heights Cyclops Prize, and *The Cycling Fish*, winner of
the coveted Golden Goat.

THE
FATEFUL
VOYAGE
TRADING Co